ZARIF'S
CONVENIENT
QUEEN

ZARIF'S CONVENIENT QUEEN

BY

LYNNE GRAHAM

First published in Great Britain 2014
by Mills & Boon, an imprint of Harlequin (UK) Limited,
Large Print edition 2014
Eton House, 18-24 Paradise Road,
Richmond, Surrey, TW9 1SR

© 2014 Lynne Graham

ISBN: 978-0-263-24125-9

Printed and bound in Great Britain
by CPI Antony Rowe, Chippenham, Wiltshire

CHAPTER ONE

ZARIF WAS BORED. The opulent attractions of his creamy-skinned and highly sophisticated mistress had palled. Right at that minute she was posed on the bed, entranced by her reflection in the mirror as she adjusted the glowing ruby pendant now encircling her throat. 'It's so beautiful,' she told him, wide-eyed with avid admiration. 'Thank you. You've been very generous.'

Lena was shrewd. She knew the pendant was a goodbye gift and that she would vacate his lavish Dubai apartment without argument and cruise off in search of another rich man. Sex, Zarif had discovered, was no big deal. He preferred amateurs to professionals in the bedroom but had few illusions about the morals of the women he took as lovers. He gave them the means to enjoy the good things in life while they gave him a necessary outlet for his highly charged sex drive. Such women understood the need for discretion and appreciated that approaching the media would be a seriously unwise career move.

And Zarif had more need than most men to conserve his public image. At the age of twelve he had become the King of Vashir with his uncle acting as Regent until Zarif attained his majority. He was the latest in a long line of feudal rulers to occupy the Emerald throne in the old palace. Vashir was oil-rich, but very conservative, and whenever Zarif tried to drag the country into the twenty-first century the old guard on his advisory council—composed of twelve tribal sheiks all over the age of sixty—panicked and pleaded with him to reconsider.

'Are you getting married?' Lena shot the question at him abruptly and then gave him a discomfited glance. 'Sorry, I know it's none of my business.'

'Not yet but soon,' Zarif responded flatly, straightening the tailored jacket of his business suit and turning on his heel.

'Good luck,' Lena breathed. 'She'll be a lucky woman.'

Zarif was still frowning as he entered the lift. When it came to marriage or children, luck didn't feature much in his family tree. Historically the love matches had fared as badly as the practical alliances and very few children had been born. Zarif had grown up an only child and he could no longer withstand the pressure on him at home to marry and provide an heir. He had only got to reach the age of twenty-nine single because he was, in fact, a widower, whose wife, Azel, and infant son, Firas, had died in a car crash seven years earlier.

At the time, Zarif had thought he would never recover from such an indescribable loss. Everyone had respected his right to grieve but even so he was well aware that he could not ignore his obligations indefinitely. Preserving the continuity of his bloodline to ensure stability in the country that he loved was his most basic duty. In truth, however, he didn't want a wife at all and he felt guilty about that. But he *liked* being alone; he *liked* his life just as it was.

A sleek private jet returned Zarif to Vashir. Before disembarking he donned the long white tunic, beige cloak and rope-bound headdress required for him to attend the ceremonial opening of a new museum in the city centre. Only after that appearance had been made would he be free to return to the old palace, a rambling property set in lush perfumed gardens. It had long since been surpassed by the giant shiny new palace built on the other side of the city, which now functioned as the official centre of government. Zarif, however, had grown up at the old palace and was strongly attached to the ancient building.

It was also where his beloved uncle, Halim, was spending the last months of his terminal illness and Zarif was making the most of the time the older man had left. In many ways, Halim had been the father whom Zarif had never known, a gentle, quiet man, who had taught Zarif everything he had needed to know about negotiation, self-discipline and statesmanship.

Zarif's business manager, Yaman, awaited him in the room Zarif used as an office. 'What brings you here?' Zarif asked in surprise for the older man rarely made such visits.

Unlike his brothers, Nik and Cristo, who had

both made names in the financial world, Zarif had little interest in his business affairs. Vashir had become oil-rich long before he was born and he had grown up wrapped in the golden cocoon of his family's fabulous wealth. Yaman and his highly professional team presided over that fortune and conserved it.

'There is a matter which I felt I should bring to your personal attention,' Yaman informed him gravely.

'Of course. What is this matter?' Zarif asked, resting back against the edge of his desk, his dark eyes enquiring in his lean bronzed features.

The middle-aged accountant's air of discomfiture increased. 'It relates to a personal loan you made to a friend three years ago…Jason Gilchrist.'

Disconcerted by the mention of that name, Zarif stiffened. Yet it was not his one-time friend's face that he pictured, it was that of Jason's sister, Eleonora. An image of a young woman with a honey-blonde fall of silky curls, gentian-blue eyes and the legs of a gazelle flashed in his mind's eye. Zarif froze into angry defensiveness at the speed of his own unwelcome response and the unwelcome remembrance of the staccato delivery of insults he had never forgotten:

We're both far too young to get married.

I'm British. I couldn't live in a culture where women are second-class citizens.

I'm not cut out to be a queen.

'What has happened?' he asked Yaman with his customary quietness, only the charge of sudden flaring energy lighting his dark gaze to amber belying his outer façade of cool.

Ella walked into the silent house. She was so tired that only will power was keeping her upright.

A light was burning below the living-room door: Jason was still up. She walked past quietly, unable to face another clash with her hot-tempered brother, and went into the kitchen. The room was a disaster area with abandoned plates of food still resting on the table. The chairs were still pushed back from the day before, when they had each leapt out of their seats as Jason broke his devastating news of their financial ruin during a family meal. Straightening her shoulders and reluctant to recall that dreadful lunch, Ella began to clear up, knowing that she would only feel worse if she had to face the mess in the morning.

The house didn't feel like home without her parents. Distressing images of her mother lying still, frail and newly old in her hospital bed, and her father sobbing uncontrollably, filled Ella's mind. Hot tears stung her eyes and she blinked them away fiercely because giving rein to self-pity and sadness wouldn't change anything that had happened.

The horrors of the past forty-eight hours had piled up like a multiple-car road crash. The night-mare had begun when Jason admitted that the family accountancy firm was on the brink of bankruptcy and that her parents' comfortable home, where they all lived together, was mort-gaged to the hilt. Only just returned from the Mediterranean cruise that Jason had persuaded his parents to take while he looked after the busi-ness, her father had been irate and incredulous that matters could have been brought to such a desperate pass in so short a time period. Gerald Gilchrist had rushed off to the office to check the firm's books and then consult his bank manager for advice while Jason stayed behind to explain the situation in greater detail to their mother.

Initially, Jennifer Gilchrist had remained calm, seemingly convinced that her clever, successful son would naturally be able to sort out whatever problems there were and ensure his family's continuing prosperity. Unlike her husband she had not angrily condemned Jason for his dishonesty in forging his parents' signatures on the document used to remortgage their home. Indeed she had forgivingly assumed that Jason had merely been trying to protect his parents from needless financial worry.

But then Jason had, from birth, been the adored centre of her parents' world, Ella conceded wryly. Excuses had always been made when Jason lied or cheated and forgiveness and instant understanding had been offered to him on many occasions. Born both brainy and athletic, Jason had shone in every sphere and her parents' pride in him had known no bounds. Yet her brother had always had a darker side to his character combined with a disturbing lack of concern for the well-being of others. Her parents had scrimped and saved to send Jason to an elite private school and when he had won a place at Oxford University they had been overjoyed by his achievement.

At university, Jason had made friends with much wealthier students. Was that when her sibling had begun to succumb to the kind of driving ambition and greed that would only lead him into trouble? Or had that change taken place only after Jason had become a high-flying banker with a Porsche and a strong sense of entitlement? Whatever it was, Ella thought with newly learned bitterness, Jason had always wanted *more* and almost inevitably that craving for easily acquired riches had tempted him down the wrong path in life. But what she would never be able to forgive her brother for was dragging their parents down with him into the mire of debt and despair.

The worst had already happened though, Ella told herself in urgent consolation. Nothing could equal the horror of her mother's collapse. Once the shock of their disastrous financial situation had finally kicked in, her mother had suffered a heart attack. Rushed into hospital the day before,

Jennifer Gilchrist had had emergency surgery and was now mercifully in the recovery ward. Her father had tried hard to adjust to his sudden change in circumstances but, ultimately, it had been too much for him once he appreciated that he would not even be able to pay his staff the wages they were owed. Shock and shame had then overwhelmed him and he had broken down in the hospital waiting room and cried in his daughter's arms, while blaming himself for not keeping a closer eye on his son's activities within the firm.

A slight noise sent Ella's head whipping round. Her brother, who had the thickset build of a rugby player and the portly outline of a man who wasted little time keeping fit, stood in the kitchen doorway nursing a glass of whisky. 'How's Mother?' he asked gruffly.

'Holding her own. The prognosis is good,' Ella told him quietly and she turned back to the sink, keen to keep busy rather than dwell on the disquieting fact that her brother had neither accompanied her to the hospital nor made the effort to visit their mother since.

'It's not my fault she had the heart attack,' Jason declared in a belligerent tone.

'I didn't say it was,' Ella responded, determined not to get into an argument with her sibling, who even as a child would have argued twenty-four hours straight sooner than yield a point. 'I'm not looking to blame anyone.'

'I mean…Mother could've had an attack at any time and at least the way it happened we were here to deal with it and ensure she got to hospital quickly,' Jason pointed out glibly.

'Yes,' Ella agreed soothingly for the sake of peace and she paused before continuing, 'I wanted to ask you…that massive loan that you said you took out three years ago…'

'What about it?' Jason prompted with a harshness that suggested that he was in no mood to answer her questions.

'Which bank was it with?'

'No bank would've given me that amount of cash without collateral,' Jason countered with a look that scorned her ignorance of such matters. 'Zarif gave me the money.'

When he spoke that name out loud, the sink

brush fell from Ella's hand as her fingers lost their grip and she whirled round from the sink in shock. *'Zarif?'* she repeated in disbelief, her voice breaking on the syllables.

'After I was made redundant at the bank, Zarif offered me the cash to start up my own business. An interest-free loan, no repayments to be made for the first three years,' Jason explained grudgingly. 'Only an idiot would have refused to take advantage of such a sweet deal.'

'That was very…kind of him,' Ella remarked tightly, her lovely face pale and tight with control while she battled the far more powerful feelings struggling inside her. Reactions she had learned to suppress during three long years of fierce self-discipline, never ever allowing herself to look back to what had been the most agonising experience of her entire life. 'But you didn't start up your own business…you became Dad's partner instead.'

'Well, home's where the heart is, or so they say,' her brother quipped without shame. 'The family firm was going nowhere until I stepped in.'

Ella bit back an angry rejoinder and compressed her lips in resolute silence. She wished Jason had chosen to set up his own business. Instead he had bankrupted a stable firm that had brought in a good, if not spectacular, income. 'I can't believe you accepted money from Zarif.'

'When a billionaire flashes his cash in my direction, I'd be a fool to do otherwise,' Jason informed her in a patronising tone. 'Of course Zarif only offered the loan in the first place because he thought you were going to marry him and an unemployed brother-in-law would have been a serious embarrassment to him.'

The muscles in Ella's slender back stretched taut as her brother voiced that unsettling claim. 'If that's true, you should've given the money back to him when we broke up.'

'You didn't break up, Ella,' Jason interrupted scornfully. 'You *inexplicably* refused to marry the catch of the century. Zarif was hardly going to come back and visit us after a slap in the face like that. So, if you're looking for someone to blame for this mess, look at the part *you* played in setting us all up for this fall!'

Blue eyes flying wide with dismay, her delicate cheekbones flushed, Ella spun round again. 'Are you trying to suggest that I'm in some way responsible for what's happened?'

Bitter resentment flared in her brother's blood-shot blue eyes. 'You made an entirely selfish decision to reject Zarif, which not only offended him but also destroyed *my* friendship with him… I mean, he never contacted me again!'

Ella lowered her pounding head, loose waves of thick honey-coloured blonde hair concealing her discomfited face and deeply troubled eyes. Her brother's friendship with Zarif *had* to all intents and purposes died the same day that Ella had refused Zarif's proposal of marriage and she could not deny that fact. 'I may have turned him down but it wasn't a selfish decision—we weren't right for each other,' she declared awkwardly, staring at a hole in the tiled floor.

'When I accepted that money from Zarif, I naturally assumed you were going to marry him and I had no worries about repaying it,' Jason argued vehemently, tossing back another unappreciative slug of his father's best whisky. 'Obviously it's *your* fault that we're in trouble now. After all you've had your share of Zarif's money too!'

Ella frowned, sharply disconcerted by that sudden accusation coming at her out of nowhere. 'What money? I never touched Zarif's money.'

'Oh, yes, you did,' Jason told her with galling satisfaction. 'When you needed the cash to go into partnership with Cathy on the shop, where do you think *I* got it from?'

Ella studied her big brother in horror. 'You told me it was your money, *your* savings!' she protested strickenly. 'Are you saying that the money came from Zarif's loan?'

'Where would I have got savings from?' Jason demanded with vicious derision. 'I was in debt to my eyeballs when I was made redundant. I had car loans, bank loans, a massive mortgage on my apartment…'

Ella was stunned by that blunt admission. After finishing college, she and her friend Cathy had opened a bookshop with a coffee area in the market town where they lived. Ella had borrowed from Jason to make her share of the investment and she made heavy monthly repayments to her brother in return for that initial financing. In fact, two and a half years on she was still as poor as a church mouse and couldn't afford to move out of her parents' house or run a car on her current share of the takings from the shop. The shop was doing well though, just not well enough to put icing on Ella's cake and offer her any luxuries. Cathy, the only child of affluent parents who owned a chain of nursing homes, was in a much more comfortable position because the shop was not her only means of support.

'You deliberately misled me,' Ella condemned shakily. 'I would never have accepted that money had I known it came from Zarif and you know it.'

'Beggars can't be choosers. You were glad enough to get the money at the time.'

'If it's true that my share of the shop investment came from Zarif's loan, then obviously I'm more involved than I appreciated.' On weak legs, Ella made that grudging concession before she sank down heavily in a chair by the kitchen table. 'But you can't seriously blame me for the fact that you've spent such a huge amount of that cash on silly superficial things like new offices and the like, and now can't repay it.'

Jason sent her a withering look of pure dislike that made her pale. 'Can't I? When I first got that money, I never expected to have to pay *any* of it back!' he told her bluntly. 'Naturally I assumed you'd marry Zarif, and if you *had* married him Zarif would never have expected me to repay the loan! If you must know, I blame you for this whole bloody nightmare. If you hadn't played ducks and drakes with Zarif and thrown his proposal back in his royal teeth, we wouldn't be in this situation now!'

Her teeth gritted, Ella jumped back out of her seat in a temper. 'That's not fair. From the moment you got that loan, you have been totally dishonest and criminally extravagant. You broke the law when you forged Mum and Dad's signatures to remortgage this house, you deceived all of us about what was really happening with the firm… Don't you *dare* try and make out that any of this is my fault!' she slung back at him in angry self-defence.

'You're *so* selfish and short-sighted!' Jason

condemned, his face reddening with fury and his fists clenching. 'You're the one who wrecked Zarif's friendship with this family and put us into this humiliating position, so you should be the one to go and see him now and ask him to give us the time to sort this out.'

'*See* him?' Ella repeated half an octave higher, her consternation at that suggestion unhidden. 'You want me to go and actually *see* Zarif?'

'Who better?' Jason queried with a curled lip. 'Men are always inclined to be more understanding when a beautiful woman asks them for a favour and Zarif wouldn't be human if the sight of a woman begging didn't give him a kick.'

Ella flushed to the roots of her hair and studied the surface of the table. Her heightened colour slowly receded while she contemplated the prospect of meeting Zarif again and her pallor was soon matched by a rolling tide of nauseous recoil from the image of *begging* Zarif for anything. 'I can't do it. I can't *bear* to see him again,' she framed between gritted teeth, ashamed that she was being forced to admit to such a weakness, such a lingering sensitivity towards something that had happened so long ago.

'Well, he's unlikely to want to see me in the circumstances but curiosity alone is sure to gain *you* an entry to the royal presence,' Jason forecast with soaring confidence. 'And you don't even have to go to that godforsaken country of his to do it. He's endowing some fancy science building at Oxford University and making a speech there the day after tomorrow.'

Her lovely face was pale and tight with strain. 'It hardly matters because I don't want to see or speak to Zarif again.'

'Not even to rescue Mummy and Daddy from this nightmare?' Jason chided unpleasantly. 'Let's face it—you're our only hope right now. And I can only hope that Zarif has a sentimental streak hidden somewhere behind that stiff upper lip of his.'

'I'm not responsible for the loan or the mortgaging of this house behind Mum and Dad's back,' Ella stated curtly while secretly wondering whether she *was* being selfish and feeling tortured by her brother's insistence that only she could help her parents in their current plight.

Was Jason only trying to manipulate her to save his own hide? Making a last-ditch suggestion that would mortify her pride but that would ultimately make no difference to the situation? Did he really think that Zarif would listen to her? Certainly, Zarif had liked and respected her mother and father and probably had no idea that Jason's mishandling of the loan had destroyed her parents' security as well as his own.

'Have you no idea how valuable so rich a friend can be? Have you no concept of what you did to *my* hopes and dreams when you turned him down?' Jason demanded with stinging bitterness. 'I could've been flying high again on the back of Zarif's support.'

'But not on the strength of your own efforts,' Ella muttered in disgust half under her breath.

'What did you say?' Jason shot at her accusingly, striding forward, red-faced rage ready to consume him.

Ella slid out of her seat and carefully avoided his aggressive stance on her passage to the door.

'Nothing…I said nothing,' she lied unsteadily. 'We're both too tired and stressed for this discussion. I'm going to bed.'

'You're a selfish, *stupid* little bitch, Ella!' Jason snarled furiously behind her. 'You could have had it all and instead what have you got? A half share in a bookshop the size of a cupboard!'

Her spine stiffened and she slowly turned. 'I also have my integrity,' she declared, lifting her chin while trying not to think about the source of the loan that had helped her to buy into the shop. But it was a thought she could not evade while she went through the motions of washing and getting into bed with the slow, heavy movements of a woman moving on automatic pilot. Exhaustion was finally overcoming her.

But even as her weary body lay heavy as lead on the mattress her thoughts marched on. Whether she liked it or not she was much more personally involved in her family's financial crash than she had thought she was. As she could not afford to pay the money back in its entirety, Zarif literally owned her half of the shop, not that she thought there was any imminent risk of a billionaire putting in a claim on a share of the venture.

Jason's other allegations had hit home even harder. It was unquestionably *her* fault that Zarif had withdrawn his friendship from the Gilchrist family. Ella's rejection had stunned and angered him and quite understandably he had never visited her home or her family again. For the very first time, Ella felt guilty about that reality. She was equally willing to credit that Jason had never expected to be forced to repay Zarif's loan because he had assumed that Ella would say 'yes' if Zarif proposed. Evidently he had guessed long before Ella had that Zarif had serious intentions towards his sister and Jason had made his plans accordingly. Had her brother spent that money recklessly because he assumed he could afford to do whatever he liked with it and would never be called to account for his behaviour?

Reluctantly, Ella acknowledged that three years earlier with his expectations of advancement soaring on the idea of Zarif marrying his sister that had most likely been Jason's outlook. In the darkness she winced, shrinking from the daunting sense of responsibility now assailing her. She was not the innocent bystander she had assumed she was in the mess that her brother had created, she conceded painfully. Her relationship with Zarif had almost certainly influenced Jason's attitude to that loan and what he subsequently chose to do with the money.

She recalled that the new offices chosen for her father's accountancy firm and the hiring of extra staff had taken place while she was still dating Zarif, which meant that Jason did have some excuse for his assumption that he would never be expected to repay the money he had borrowed.

The persistent ringing of the front door bell wakened Ella from an uneasy doze. Clambering out of bed in a panic when she realised that it was after one in the morning, she dragged on her dressing gown and hurried to answer the door.

Her father's best friend, Jonathan Scarsdale, stood on the doorstep and immediately apologised for getting her out of bed. 'Your landline was constantly engaged and I thought it would be better to talk to you in person.'

Ella glanced at the phone table and noticed the

handset wasn't set on the charger and sighed because it was little wonder that the phone wasn't working.

'No…no, don't worry about that,' Ella urged, for her parents' best friends, Jonathan and Marsha, were also Cathy's parents and familiar to her from childhood. 'I'm glad to see you. Come in.'

'Perhaps I'd better,' the older man said heavily. 'Although I hate bringing you more bad news than you've already had.'

'Mum?' Ella gasped, jumping to conclusions and wide-eyed with apprehension.

'No, Ella. Your mother's fine,' Jonathan reassured her quietly. 'But your father called me from the hospital. He was so upset, I drove over to join him although there's little enough I can do to help in the current circumstances.'

Ella was pale with strain as she led the way into the lounge, switching on lights as she went. 'I'm sure Dad was grateful for you being there.'

'I'm here to talk to you about your father,' the older man told her heavily. 'I'm afraid he's having a breakdown, Ella. Jason's betrayal of his trust, your mother's heart attack, the whole situation… Unfortunately he's not able to cope with it all right now. I phoned Marsha and she came out to the hospital to speak to your father and make a professional diagnosis. She suggested that Gerald should stay in our nursing home here for a few days until he's calmed down and come to terms with things…'

'Dad…a *breakdown*?' Ella repeated sickly. 'But he's not the type.'

'There *is* no type, Ella. Anyone can have an emotional breakdown and at the moment your father simply can't handle the stress he's under. He's in the best place for the present with trained staff able to offer the support he needs,' he pointed out soothingly. 'I'm sorry though that this leaves you alone.'

'I'm not alone…I have Jason,' she pointed out, avoiding the older man's compassionate look out of embarrassment while struggling to absorb the news of her father's predicament.

Ella was shell shocked as she thanked Cathy's father for his help and she got back into bed in a daze, gooseflesh prickling at the disturbing real-isation that *both* her parents had collapsed from the trauma of Jason's revelations. There was no room for manoeuvre or protest now, she acknowledged dully. If she could do anything at all to alleviate the crisis in her parents' lives, she needed to make the attempt to do so: she had no choice but to ask Zarif for a meeting.

CHAPTER TWO

ELLA PARKED HER mother's car with the extreme care of someone strung up tight with nerves and terrified of making a mistake at the wheel.

Earlier that morning she had visited both her parents and that had proved a disorientating experience. On medication her father was now much calmer but he had seemed utterly divorced from the events that had led to his breakdown in the first place, not once even referring to them. In any case she had been warned before her visit not to touch on any subject that might cause him distress. Luckily Gerald's overriding source of concern had been his wife's recovery and he had lamented his inability to be with her. At least Ella had been able to tell her father that her mother was out of Intensive Care and receiving visits from her friends. Jennifer Gilchrest, however, had been equally reluctant to discuss the events that had preceded her heart attack.

As a result, Ella had been left feeling totally bereft of support and she was still guiltily reproaching herself for being so selfish. After all, neither of her parents was well enough to assist her. At the same time, Ella remained horribly aware of the huge burden of expectation resting on her shoulders while bankruptcy and repossession threatened her parents' business and home. She had already fielded several excusably angry phone calls from staff members who hadn't received their salary and who were struggling to pay their bills. In the midst of catastrophe, and in spite of being their father's partner in the firm, Jason had done absolutely nothing beyond contacting another former student friend to establish where Zarif was staying prior to delivering his speech at the university. Jason had then contacted the hotel on the evening of Zarif's arrival, had spoken to his chief aide and had been granted an appointment.

Jason had then made some wildly opportunistic and slick forecasts about the likely result of his sister speaking to Zarif in person.

'Zarif's really hot on family values, so he'll be very sympathetic when he appreciates how devastating all this has been for us,' Jason had opined optimistically. 'I'm tremendously relieved that you've decided to see sense about this.'

'Don't you think that you should be coming with me?' Ella had asked in surprise for she had certainly originally assumed that her brother would, at least, be accompanying her to the meeting. 'I mean, Zarif made the loan to you, not to me, and I won't be able to answer any business queries he has.'

'Take it from me. You're the best messenger the family could have,' Jason had insisted.

Only, unhappily, Ella did not feel equal to that challenge. She was painfully aware that any slight regard Zarif might have cherished for her three years earlier had died the same day she refused to marry him. Determined not to reveal her true feelings after he put her on the spot and demanded an explanation for her refusal, she had employed lame excuses, which had not only offended him but which still made her cringe in remembrance. Could she really blame him for his anger that day?

Zarif al-Rastani was born of royalty and was scarcely the average male. She might often have overlooked that reality when he was visiting them in the UK and displaying few of the trappings of his true status, but the day she had said 'no' Zarif had regarded her with stunned disbelief and his extremely healthy ego had visibly recoiled from the affront of her rejection.

Of course, he had said and done nothing that could be remotely termed *emotional* that day. Evidently Zarif didn't *do* emotion and she would have been far too emotional a being to make him a good wife, she reflected wryly. She had been sadly mistaken when she once naively assumed that Zarif's icy reserve and self-discipline masked powerful inner feelings that he preferred to keep to himself.

While she had fallen madly in love with Zarif and had craved him with every fibre of her being, she had recognised the very last time that she saw him that he was virtually indifferent to her and was not in love, merely in *lust* and in need of a male heir. Had Jason only realised how shallow her former relationship with Zarif had ultimately proved to be, he would not have been so hopeful that by some miracle his sister would somehow be able to save her family from the consequences of his extravagance. Indeed Ella suspected that Zarif was more likely to be annoyed than appreciative at her daring to request another meeting with him. Women were gentle nurturing motherly creatures in Zarif's world and that kind of woman was his ideal, as Ella knew to her cost.

She walked into the imposing country house hotel. Jason had told her that Zarif and his entourage were occupying the entire top floor of the building.

'Miss Gilchrist?' A slim Arab man with a goatee beard was on the lookout for her before she even got to engage with the reception staff. 'I am Hamid, the King's chief aide. I spoke to your brother on the phone. His Majesty will see you upstairs.'

While Hamid talked valiantly about the weather, his efforts undimmed by her monosyllabic replies,

Ella smoothed damp palms down over her long skirt, wishing she had had a smart business suit to don in place of her usual more casual clothing but she didn't own any formal outfits. She had teamed the skirt with a pristine white layered blouse and camisole. At least, she wasn't wearing jeans, she told herself in consolation, desperate to think about anything other than the approaching challenge of an interview with Zarif. Her heart started to beat very, very fast, a chill of nervous tension shivering through her slender frame and making her tummy flip. She breathed in, slow and deep, striving to calm herself.

'Miss Gilchrist...' Hamid announced, pushing wide the door.

Ella walked a few steps into the room and then saw *him* and her courage failed her and she came to a sudden halt. Six feet two inches tall with a lean, powerful build, Zarif was a stunningly beautiful male and, in her opinion, far and away the most handsome of the three half-brothers. He was also the youngest of the trio, the other two of whom she had met briefly.

Zarif had the tawny eyes of a lion framed

between lush black lashes and set deep below straight ebony brows. An arrogant, slim-bridged nose dissected exotically high cheekbones and his stunning features were completed by a strong masculine jaw line and a perfectly modelled mouth, the very thought of which had once kept Ella lying awake at night. She had craved his touch like a life-giving drug.

The memory sent chagrined heat surging through her tense body as she remembered all too well how frustrated she had become with his hands-off courtship. She had been a virgin but she would have surrendered her innocence any time he asked and if she was *still* a virgin, she conceded with undeniable resentment, it was only because she was determined not to settle for anything less than the intense hunger that Zarif had once inspired in her.

'Eleonora…' Zarif murmured, his rich as dark chocolate deep drawl dancing down her spine like the brush of ghostly fingers from the past. He did not have a definable accent because he had learned English from his British grandmother.

Her throat convulsed. 'Zarif…' she responded, struggling to push his name past her lips.

Zarif surveyed her with razor-edged intensity, luxuriant black lashes covertly veiling his acute gaze. He'd had an antique storybook as a child, which featured a lovely pale-haired princess imprisoned in a tower, and had once idly wondered if that had been the mysterious source of his one-time obsession with Ella Gilchrist. She was a beauty of the pure English Rose type with her translucent porcelain skin, bright blue eyes and long waving hair that had the depth and gloss of rich golden honey. Slim and of medium height, she had surprisingly lush curves for her slight frame and she moved as gracefully as a dancer. He scrutinised her soft bee-stung pink mouth and his body betrayed him with an immediate reaction. Anger stirred along with the indignity of the prickling heaviness of arousal at his groin.

She had always contrived to look natural, unadorned, *untouched*. His even white teeth ground together at that improbability. It had probably only ever been part of the demure fawn act she had staged for his benefit in the days when he had been that credulous and impressionable with the female sex, he reflected with angry resentment.

Time would have moved on for her in any case, just as it had done for him, and he refused to think further along that line because it would cross the bitter defensive boundaries he had raised inside his mind. After all, it was purely due to Ella Gilchrist's power over him that Zarif had later betrayed every principle he had once respected, and he still reeled from any recollection of the mistakes he had made and the very large dent inflicted on his once stainless sense of honour. She had embarked on a dangerous power game with him. She had played him like a fish on a line, vainly determined to get the ego boost of having royalty propose marriage to her without ever considering acceptance as a viable possibility.

He had considered the matter many times and believed that was the only practical explanation for her behaviour.

'Won't you sit down?' Zarif invited smoothly, his outer assurance absolute. 'Then you can tell me how I may be of assistance.'

So, Zarif was going to play dumb, Ella reckoned uncomfortably and then wondered if she was being unjust. Was it possible that he hadn't a clue about the situation her family was in?

She settled into a high-backed, opulently upholstered armchair and went straight to the heart of the subject. 'Until this week, I had no idea that three years ago you gave Jason a very large loan.'

'It was not your concern,' Zarif fielded without skipping a beat.

Ella stiffened defensively. 'But I wish it had been,' she fenced back, refusing to be intimidated by his powerful presence. 'Giving Jason a million pounds without any form of supervision was the equivalent of putting a fox in charge of a hen coop.'

Zarif compressed his handsome mouth. 'You are not very loyal to your brother.'

'I wonder how loyal you would feel towards one of your brothers if his wheeling and dealing had plunged your father's firm into bankruptcy and left your parents facing homelessness. Right now, I'm worried about them, *not* about my brother,' Ella spelt out combatively.

A gleam of surprise lightened Zarif's spectacular eyes for it had been a very long time since anyone had addressed him with such a pronounced lack of respect. Indeed the last to do so had probably been her and he was both aggravated and yet strangely entertained by her boldness. It was a complete novelty in his world, where almost every word addressed to him was wrapped in flattery and a desire to ingratiate and please. His jaw line squared. 'I was not aware that your parents were involved in this debacle.'

'They were very much involved the moment Jason became a partner in Dad's firm. My father was so proud that his son was joining the family business that he gave Jason a completely free hand,' Ella explained heavily.

'My business manager has already presented me with a file covering his investigation into how the loan was utilised,' Zarif revealed gently.

'So, really it wasn't very nice of you to ask *how* you might be of assistance when I arrived!' Ella shot back at him with spirit. 'You were being facetious at my expense.'

'Was I?' Zarif quipped, scanning the animated

expressiveness of her exquisite face, which openly brandished every emotion she experienced. He was convinced he could now read her like a children's book and recognise her angry resentment and mortification that she should be put in the position of pleading her unworthy brother's cause.

Zarif, in point of fact, had very few illusions about his former friend's character. Long ago, Zarif had slowly been repelled by the traits he saw in Jason and would have dropped the friendship much sooner had it not been for the draw of Ella's presence in the same house. His dark gaze hardened when he thought of the day it had all ended and the persistent bite of his indignation and dissatisfaction stung his ferocious pride afresh, tensing his spectacular bone structure and settling the charismatic curve of his mouth into a hard stubborn line. She had humiliated him, insulted his country and his people and outraged him beyond forgiveness but torture would not have persuaded him to admit that reality.

'I think so,' Ella told him squarely, noting the way his long dark lashes shadowed his cheekbones when he glanced down at her, seeing his handsome dark head take on a familiar angle, recalling how he had once listened to her with just that attitude. Unnerved by the memory and the overpowering urge to stare and eat up his heartbreaking gorgeousness without restraint, Ella glanced furiously in the direction of the window like someone calculating the chances of her escape.

Unbelievable as it now seemed, she had once loved Zarif with her whole heart and soul, she recalled painfully. She would have done absolutely anything for him and in return he had *hurt* her very badly, inflicting a wound and an insecurity that even the passage of three long years had failed to eradicate. Even so, it had been a novel experience to discover that a marriage proposal could actually be wielded like an offensive weapon.

'When I gave that loan to Jason, it was in the true spirit of generosity,' Zarif countered with quiet assurance. 'He was devastated by the loss of his employment and your parents were equally upset on his behalf. I genuinely wanted to help your family.'

'That may be so,' Ella conceded uncomfortably, because he seemed sincere, 'but nothing is ever that simple. Jason needed another job more than he needed that cash. The loan just tempted him into dangerous fantasies about building his own business empire.'

'As well as the settling of his personal debts, which was dishonest and in direct conflict with the terms on which the loan was made,' Zarif sliced in calmly, cold censure of such behaviour etched in his lean bronzed features. 'Your brother squandered the bulk of the money on frivolous purchases, which included a new Porsche and a personalised Range Rover. I will not write off the debt and forgive it. It would be against my principles to overlook what amounts to fraudulent behaviour.'

'That is all very well, but what about my parents' position in all this?' Ella demanded emotively. 'Do they deserve to suffer for Jason's mistakes?'

'That is not for me to answer,' Zarif responded without expression. 'They raised Jason, taught him their values. They must know their son best.'

'No.' Ella challenged that view with vehement force. 'They only know the man they *wanted* him to be, not the man he actually is! At this moment, my mother and father are distraught at what Jason's done.'

An untimely knock on the door at that instant of high tension heralded the appearance of a waiter with a tray. Ella closed her lips and breathed in deep to master her tumultuous emotions. Coffee was served in fine china cups, cakes proffered. Any appetite Ella might have had following her scratch meals in recent days had been killed stone dead by her ever-growing sense of dread of what the future might yet visit on her parents. In the lingering silence while the waiter walked to the door to leave, she searched Zarif's extravagantly handsome features, cursing his inscrutability, desperate to see some sign of a softer response to her appeal on her parents' behalf.

'I'm afraid I don't understand what you want from me,' Zarif murmured half under his breath, his temperature rising as she sat forward, inadvertently revealing the shadowy valley between her full rounded breasts. There was a bitter irony to his response for he knew in that moment of fierce driving desire that what he wanted from her was exactly what he was convinced he could have had for the asking three years earlier.

Back then he had been no sophisticate, having never slept with anyone other than the wife he had married at the age of eighteen. He had wanted Ella and she had wanted him but he had believed it would be dishonourable to become intimate with her before he married her. Thanks to Ella's rejection, he was no longer that innocent, he reflected with a bitterness that was laced with regret for past mistakes. His wide sensual mouth narrowed and compressed while he wondered if she was deliberately playing the temptress as women so often did with him in an effort to divert and attract him.

'No, you are not that stupid,' Ella flung back at him feelingly, pushing her slender hands down on the arms of the chair to rise upright and confront him. 'You know very well I'm asking you to show some compassion for my parents' predicament.'

The swishing luxuriance of her golden hair as

it swung round her shoulders engaged his scrutiny, which lingered to take in the rosy colour warming her delicate features, serving only to accentuate the sapphire brilliance of her eyes. 'In what way? And what are you offering me in return?' Zarif murmured very drily. 'Do you not think that in the complete loss of that loan, I have already paid dearly for my act of generosity towards your family?'

Confronted with that blunt question, Ella felt her face burn as though he had slapped it hard because that was not an angle she could take into account when she was asking him for yet another favour. 'Yes, you have paid dearly…we all have, but I do genuinely believe that you should have thought about what you were doing when you offered Jason that loan in the first place.'

'Before you start blaming me for your brother's dishonesty and awakening my anger,' Zarif purred like a jungle cat, shimmering dark golden eyes settling on her with predatory force and shocking her into sudden silence, 'think about what you are saying and what you are asking me for. Some form of forgiveness which, as I have already stated, is out of the question in this case? Or are you asking me to throw away more money on your family?'

Standing there, Ella turned very pale, shame and anxiety combining to stir nausea in her tummy. Her tongue was glued to the roof of her mouth. She absolutely got his point and she could not bring herself to outright *ask* him for money to aid her parents because that seemed so very wrong, indeed quite outrageous in the circumstances. For the first time she questioned why she had approached him in the first place and why she had allowed Jason to influence her attitude. Surely, had she taken the time to think things through, she would have recognised that to ask Zarif for further financial help would be indefensible?

'I'm just asking you to show some compassion, not for Jason or me but for my parents,' she completed limply, too mortified to even make an attempt to meet his slashing gaze, knowing that it would only intensify her awareness of the weak and humiliating role she had allowed her brother to browbeat her into accepting. For an instant, she almost burst into speech about her parents' current health problems, but compressed her lips on the conviction that playing a thousand violins to invite Zarif's pity would only shame her and her family more.

'Nicely put,' Zarif countered with sardonic bite, his dark eyes glittering like jet knives, so shrewd was the stab of his incisive gaze. 'You know how wealthy I am and like many other people I have met you expect me to come to the rescue. And I would have to ask you, especially when you have the audacity to ask me to go against my principles, what am I to receive in payment?'

The suffocating tension was convulsing Ella's dry throat. She turned away, dropped down into her seat again and lifted her coffee cup like a tiny shield. 'In payment? Anything I can offer,' she muttered unevenly, knowing she had nothing to offer but gratitude and seriously embarrassed by that reality.

'Are you offering me sex?' Zarif enquired lazily.

And for a split second in receipt of that shocking question Ella wondered if she would agree to such a belittling act of intimacy if it could magically return her parents' lives to normal. The answer came fast and forthright in her mind. And colour surged across her cheeks and ran up in a tide of pink to her hairline while her coffee cup rattled on the saucer as her hand trembled.

'I can get sex anywhere whenever I want,' Zarif derided.

'I wasn't going to offer it,' Ella told him with as much dignity as she could muster, her teeth gritting on his arrogant self-assurance. Nevertheless, she suspected that he was simply stating the situation as it was. He was exceptionally good-looking and shockingly rich even without considering the kick it would give some women to bed a reigning king. She was quite sure that willing women formed queues for the privilege of getting him into bed and her staunch conviction that he was a virtually irresistible package only incensed her more.

Surprisingly for a male so well aware of the high currency value of sex, Zarif believed Ella because he couldn't credit that a truly sophisticated woman would still blush the way she did.

But the imagery in his mind was far from sophisticated and he knew from the intensely male burn of his rapidly awakening libido that if she *had* offered, he would have said yes and to hell with whether or not such ignoble behaviour would be beneath him!

That discovery shook him because while sex was easily available to Zarif and an appetite he could not ignore, he had never viewed it as a special or even greatly prized pleasure. But for some reason when he looked at Ella Gilchrist his body hummed with the expectation of *extraordinary* pleasure because it was the passion in her volatile nature that had drawn him to her from the first. He crushed that exciting fantasy at source, reminding himself that he needed a wife and a child much more than he needed a passionate mistress.

On that thought, he stiffened, unable to overlook the reality that had she said yes when he asked her to marry him he most likely would have been a father again by now. All the old dark anger and bitterness he had buried stirred deep inside him once more, razor-edged thoughts of his unresolved desire for her taunting his ferocious pride.

He had never wanted a woman as much as he had once wanted Ella Gilchrist and she was the only woman he had ever desired whom he had not enjoyed. Perhaps that was the secret of her persistent attraction, he reasoned with inherent self-loathing at the concept of such a personal weakness, and it would naturally follow that familiarity would soon breed contempt. That conviction soothed him, offering as it did the promise that in the future he would forget about her and the way she had once adversely affected him. Life was too short for regrets and 'what ifs'. He would get bored with her. He *always* got bored in the end because women could be very predictable. She would be his very last rebellion against the staid and respectable married future that awaited him. He would have some fun and *then* he would do his duty by settling down again with a wife and having children, he swore to himself.

'That's unfortunate,' Zarif responded in reply to her proud declaration that she had not been offering him sex. 'Because what you say you would not offer is the only thing that I want from you.'

Extreme disconcertion slithered through Ella while she mentally unpicked his words several times to persuade herself that she had not misunderstood his meaning. He was telling her that he still found her attractive and that the only thing he wanted from her was sex? How dared he admit that with such smooth and utterly shameless cool? Heat warmed her cheeks afresh and speared down between her breasts as she bit back furious words of reproach and fought to breathe normally.

'I can't believe you can say that to me.'

'Duplicity would be of little use to you at this point,' Zarif countered quietly. 'Whatever else I may be guilty of, you can trust me to always tell you the truth.'

For an instant, Ella froze, recalling the last unforgettable occasion when he had told her the truth that he did not love her and would *never* love her: a hauntingly savage moment that had coloured her every memory of him with pain and a deep sense of humiliation. She had often thought that lies would have been kinder, only then she would have married him and ultimately would have ended up being very unhappy.

'I want you in my bed,' Zarif admitted with unblemished cool. 'In return I would ensure that your parents' financial status is restored to what it was before Jason's mismanagement ruined their security.'

I want you in my bed. A tingling sensation curled like a tongue of flame low in her pelvis and Ella shifted uneasily on her seat, trying not to imagine what it would be like to share Zarif's bed. Wide-eyed and hot inside skin that suddenly felt tight over her bones, she focused on the undoubtedly handmade leather shoes on his feet and kept her ready tongue clamped firmly between her teeth. She was fighting her own natural instincts harder with every second that passed. She could have asked him if he was joking and instantly rejected such a shocking proposition. She could have made a scene and stormed out in an impressive temper. But Ella had a strong streak of caution and practicality and she was all too well aware that Zarif al-Rastani was the only possible individual in a position to help her family.

'That's immoral,' she declared half under her breath, unable to resist making that accusation. 'You're inviting me to sell myself to you.'

'I'm offering you the only rescue bid you're likely to receive. It is for you to choose whether or not you will accept my proposition,' Zarif contradicted, shutting out every protest emanating from his clean-living conservative soul and refusing to listen. One final act of rebellion, he reminded himself doggedly. And didn't she deserve it for the games she had played three years back when she had lured him in with the promise of her passion and her beautiful body and falsely encouraged him to believe that she genuinely cared for him?

'How long would you envisage this…arrangement lasting for?' Ella prompted, her voice high and tight with strain for she could barely credit that after three years apart she could even be having such a conversation with him.

'A year…' Zarif murmured, disconcerted by the speed with which that time period had suggested itself to him and wondering where that idea had come from. After all, he had never kept a single mistress for as long as a year. His interest in a woman faded within the first few weeks of bedding her even though he saw comparatively little of his lovers. At the same time he tried and failed to picture Ella in the Dubai apartment while wondering if word of an Englishwoman's presence there would be more likely to be leaked to the press. Just as quickly, he realised that the Dubai option would be a very bad idea. And that indeed he had a much better idea in the offing and one indeed that would make the punishment fit the crime.

'For the sake of appearances, we will get married,' Zarif decreed without hesitation.

'Married?' Ella exclaimed with stark incredulity.

'I don't want a scandal and if I marry you, even when it ends in divorce after a year, it will be a safer and more acceptable option to my people. Marriage would also have the advantage of allowing me to see as much of you as I want to,' Zarif completed smoothly, his mind made up, the stirrings of his conscience magically washed away. If he married her, after all, he wouldn't be breaking any rules or taking advantage of her. It was wonderful, he thought with a rare lightness of heart, what a little thinking outside the box could achieve.

Feeling rather as though she had gone ten rounds with a champion boxer, Ella stood up and set down her coffee cup. Marry Zarif? Embrace all that she had rejected three years earlier? Her entire being shrank from such a challenge. 'I couldn't do it...I *couldn't* marry you.'

Raw anger roared like a hurricane through Zarif's lean powerful frame and gleamed pure, startlingly bright gold in his tawny eyes. 'You have twelve hours in which to consider that position,' he breathed in a raw-edged undertone. 'If you don't phone me within that period, I will assume that the negative answer stands.'

Ella's feet were locked to the carpet, her eyes flying wide on his hard, darkly handsome features. Dismay was piercing her with little warning stabs and reminding her that rejecting her parents' only rescue option was not a good idea.

'Twelve hours is ridiculous,' she said nonetheless, playing for time.

'It is more than generous,' Zarif contradicted.

Ella was pale as a white sheet. 'Even when you know you've already won?' she whispered, because all the pros and cons were piling up like an avalanche inside her brain and she could not evade the obvious answer.

Zarif could turn the clock back for her parents, returning their lives to the safe cosy routine that had been theirs before Jason's interference. Zarif was the only person with the power to do that. Her father's staff would also be protected from unemployment. How could she possibly turn her back on such important results and walk away, leaving her parents and everybody else concerned to sink or swim? All the cons, after all, would be on *her* side of the fence, making the payment one of personal sacrifice.

Zarif stalked closer with all the grace of a prowling black panther. *'Have I won?'*

'How could I turn down an offer like that?' Ella asked shakily. 'My parents don't deserve what they're going through right now. It's bad enough for them to be forced to face the kind of person Jason really is without facing financial ruin at the same time.'

Zarif stretched out a slim tanned hand and closed it round hers to tug her closer. 'So, you *will* marry me?'

'But it won't work…even for only a year,' Ella protested weakly. 'I won't fit in.'

Eyes golden as the heart of a fire flamed over her troubled face. 'You will fit in my bed to perfection,' Zarif assured her and as panic and sexual awareness clenched her every muscle with raw tension Ella registered that that was really the *only* thought in his mind.

She stared up at him, almost mesmerised by his stunning gaze, and he lowered his head. His wide sensual mouth nuzzled against the corner of hers and she shivered, suddenly hot and cold inside her skin while little tingles of sexual awareness snaked through the lower part of her body. The scent of him was in her nostrils, a hint of some exotic spice overlaid with clean, husky male that was both familiar and dangerously welcome. His wide mobile mouth drifted across hers, his tongue breaking the seal of her lips and darting within, plunging deep in a single measured stab of eroticism before he pressed his hard mouth urgently to hers. That kiss was like being hit with white lightning, desire exploding within her like a fire ball, fiery tendrils of heat reaching low in her belly, and her knees trembled, her breasts swelling and nipples pinching tight.

Zarif lifted his handsome dark head and slowly drew in a deep breath to look down at her with hot possessive appreciation blazing in his golden eyes. 'Yes, you will fit into my bed as though you were born to be there.'

In the aftermath, rage gripped Ella and she wanted to smack him across the face. For a split second she had lost control, indeed lost sight of everything because he had thrown her straight into that disturbing world of exciting sensation that she had almost forgotten. And she could have wept at that knowledge for she had diligently dated more than one attractive man over the past three years and not one of them had made her heart leap and her body tremble with a single kiss. At the same time she had no doubt that that brief embrace had affected Zarif on a much less high-flown level.

'No, I wasn't born to be in your bed…Azel was,' Ella murmured flatly.

Disconcerted by the mere mention of Azel's name, Zarif froze and shot an icy look of censure down at her. 'You will not mention the name of my late wife or that of our child ever again,' he warned her forbiddingly.

Well, at least she didn't need to have any doubts about exactly where she stood in her future husband's affections, Ella reflected grimly. But then that had been exactly why she *didn't* marry the man she had once loved. Even seven years after her passing, Azel still ruled Zarif's heart.

CHAPTER THREE

'No,' ELLA TOLD her brother with quiet determination. 'If you want to ask Zarif anything, *you* go and see him.'

'And what use is that going to be? For goodness' sake, you're *marrying* the guy!' Jason reminded her angrily. 'Obviously you've got more sway with him than anyone else. Mum and Dad are over the moon and everything in everybody's garden but mine is coming up roses. What about *me*?'

Ella studiously averted her gaze from her sibling's furious face. Over the past three weeks everything had changed within the family circle. Once her father had heard his daughter's news, he had made a steady recovery and had gratefully accepted Zarif's contention that he could hardly let his future wife's family either go bankrupt or lose their home. Zarif's business manager,

Yaman, had booked into a local hotel and the two men had worked out a viable rescue plan for the ailing firm. But right from that first day, all financial assistance on offer had been subject to the assurance that Jason would resign from the partnership and that her father would promise not to hire him again in any capacity. Gerald Gilchrist had duly given those guarantees and Jason had now officially left the firm. Her father had also insisted that Zarif's aid be given in the form of a loan, which he intended to start repaying as soon as he could.

'I'm sorry, Jason,' Ella breathed uncomfortably. 'Zarif isn't a forgiving person.'

'I'm out of a job and Dad thinks it would be easier all round if I move out of this house before your bloody ridiculous wedding!' Jason snapped out resentfully. 'What am I supposed to do?'

'Look for a career that suits you. Something that isn't financially orientated,' Ella suggested ruefully.

Her brother stomped off. Ella's mother, Jennifer, emerged from the kitchen and winced at the slam of a door overhead. 'Thank you for taking the heat off me and your father. I don't have the patience to listen to Jason's bitter rants right now and I don't want him making your father feel guilty again,' she confided.

The older woman had lost weight since her heart attack, which was hardly surprising if one considered her mother's new walking regime and healthier diet, Ella acknowledged fondly, relieved and proud of the way her mother had adapted to the challenge of changing her lifestyle.

'I'm *so* looking forward to the wedding,' Jennifer admitted happily. 'It's wonderful to have something to smile about again.'

And that was her parents' attitude to her nuptials in a nutshell, Ella conceded wryly. They thought it was wonderful news that she was marrying Zarif. She had lied to them and they hadn't suspected a thing was amiss. She had told them that she had turned down Zarif's first proposal because she didn't feel up to the challenge of the public role he was offering her and they had completely understood and accepted that explanation. In the same way it had been quite easy to persuade the older couple that once Zarif and their daughter had met again, they had recognised that their feelings were unchanged and had reconciled while deciding to waste no further time in getting married.

Ella's personal feelings were exactly that: *strictly* personal. Jason, of course, who thought everybody thought the way he did, assumed she was marrying Zarif for his money. And, of course, in a twisted way, she *was* marrying him for his money, Ella acknowledged shamefacedly. Marriage was the price of protecting her parents from a nasty wake-up call at an age when they no longer had the time and strength to deal with such a colossal challenge. Ella was, however, willing and able to pay that price for the mother and father who had surrounded her with love from the day of her birth. As a boy, Jason might have been the favourite but Ella had never been short-changed when it came to parental care and attention.

The phone rang and her mother, still mistily smiling at the prospect of her daughter's wedding, which was only three days away, answered it. 'The wedding planner,' she said, passing the receiver straight over to Ella.

Ella breathed in deep. Zarif had instructed his aide, Hamid, to put all the wedding arrangements in the hands of a top-flight professional, able to work to a very tight schedule and stage the wedding within weeks. A fixed smile tightening her tense lips, Ella listened to the planner's dilemma on whether the napkins should be purple or plum in colour before admitting that she didn't care which colour was chosen.

'You're the most easy-going bride I've ever worked for,' the planner told her and not for the first time.

No, Ella was simply an unwilling bride, who, while prepared to play along with appearances for the sake of her parents, refused to pretend otherwise when it came to all the bridal decisions. A woman in love would want everything perfect and would have her own ideas. But Ella was not in love and no longer the dreaming romantic girl she had been at the age of twenty-one when she had fantasised about walking down the aisle clad in blinding white to greet Zarif.

She had taken the phone into the drawing room, which her parents only used when they entertained. As she hovered there she remembered her twenty-first birthday and the night when Zarif had first deigned to notice that she was alive and female. To her surprise, he had come to her party and he had given her a very pretty contemporary silver necklace and matching bracelet. Her heart had been hammering fit to burst while he stood there chatting to her and when he had invited her out for a meal the following evening, virtually announcing his new interest in her, it had been like her every dream coming true at once.

It was ironic, she had often thought, that Azel had been Zarif's first love and that Zarif had then become Ella's. Nobody knew better than Ella how desperately hard it was to shake free of the trappings of adolescent fantasy. Zarif had first come into her life when she was only seventeen and she had taken one dazed look at him and fallen like a ton of bricks. At that time, he had given her not the smallest encouragement. His eyes hadn't lingered on her, he hadn't flirted with her and he had never been alone with her but

Ella had still lived for the weekends that Jason brought Zarif home with him. The boys her own age who paid attention to her had seemed like immature kids in comparison to Zarif, who had spent five years in his country's army as a soldier before he came to the UK to study for a physics degree. His spectacular good looks, wonderful manners and exotic background had enthralled her.

On their first date he had kissed her and a whole other level of attraction had surged through her in response. She had felt things she had never felt before; she had felt her whole body light up like a blazing torch in his arms and afterwards that had become the bar other men had had to reach to impress her. Only none of them ever had, she conceded reluctantly. And that last kiss, the one in his hotel suite, had proved that Zarif still had the power to make her want to rip his clothes off. Uneasy with that reality, Ella paced the floor.

She had only spoken to Zarif a handful of times on the phone since she had agreed to marry him. He had returned to Vashir while she had been busy running after her parents, dealing with the wedding planner and persuading Cathy to hire someone to take her place rather than asking Ella to sell her share of the business to her. At least she would still have the shop to come home to in a year's time, she reflected ruefully.

Would it even take a year for Zarif to decide that he had had his revenge and was now bored with it and her? What else could possibly be motivating him? She was the woman who had said no and evidently her value in his estimation had leapt sky-high at the same moment. She was convinced that had he slept with her three years earlier, he would no longer have wanted her. But what drove him hardest? Sexual hunger or a need for revenge?

Three years earlier he had been icily outraged by her gauche foot-in-the-mouth refusal of his proposal. He hadn't been prepared for it, hadn't foreseen that even though she was in love with him she had had doubts about whether she could successfully live in his world. So, although she had worded her misgivings clumsily and insulted him, her concerns had been genuine, and layered over the disappointment of learning that he had buried any ability to become emotionally attached to a woman in the grave with his first wife and child.

It totally amazed her that Zarif's desire for her body could act as such a powerful incentive on him. How would he react when she proved inexperienced in his precious bed? Was sex really that important to him? And to offer her marriage on such a score? That was crazy, she thought ruefully, particularly as he presumably had no intention of working to establish a normal marital relationship with her. After all, in a year at most it would be over and she would be a divorcee back at home with her disappointed parents, probably using the excuse that her marriage had broken down because it had just been too difficult to surmount the differences between them in background and culture.

A year was such a short time, she told herself, surely it would pass quickly. Though a split second later she conceded that time never passed quickly though when you were unhappy. She would just have to hope that Zarif was prepared to put more effort into being married to her than his approach had so far suggested…

'You need to get up,' Cathy urged Ella, shaking her awake from a deep dreamless sleep.

Ella looked up drowsily at her best friend, a blonde with a spiky short haircut and bright brown eyes that were currently frowning. She was bemused by her tone of urgency. Cathy had stayed over and they had sat up late relaxing and talking. 'What time is it?'

'Only seven,' Cathy confided ruefully. 'My father came over with the morning papers and then the phone started ringing and that four-letter word has really hit the fan.'

Ella sat up and grabbed her dressing gown. 'What are you talking about? It *is* my wedding day…isn't it?' she queried in a daze.

'You should go downstairs. I'll be tactful and stay up here,' her friend told her uncomfortably. 'My dad's already gone home. There's an utterly preposterous story about you in the newspaper and your parents are upset. There's also a pack of photographers standing out on the drive and

I think one of them has his finger stuck in the doorbell. I don't know how you've slept through it all.'

'Blame the large glasses of wine we shared. A story about me? *Photographers?* What on earth?' Ella exclaimed, blundering into the bathroom to steal a moment in which to freshen up before starting down the stairs, noting that the curtains were still pulled in the lounge and also over the glass-panelled front door, cocooning the house in dimness. The phone was off the hook and the doorbell was ringing but seemingly being ignored.

There was a deathly hush inside the kitchen where a newspaper was spread open on the table. Her mother was mopping tears from her reddened eyes and her father was tense and flushed with annoyance.

'What on earth has happened?' Ella whispered.

'Read that,' her father told her, directing a look of angry revulsion at the newspaper.

It was a double-page spread in the *Daily Shout*, the most downmarket tabloid sold in the UK, and generally full of celebrity exposés of cheating married men and women. Scandals sold newspapers but Ella could think of absolutely nothing in her own life, aside of her upwardly mobile wedding plans, which could possibly have attracted such salacious media attention. She froze by the table, recognising the photos scattered at random across the article.

'Where did they get those photos?' she demanded in consternation, because they were *family* photos. There was one of her aged eighteen wearing a bikini on a Spanish beach holiday, another of her as a fair-haired toddler in her mother's arms, yet another of her aged about ten in school uniform.

'Jason must've taken them from the albums in the trunk in our bedroom,' Jennifer Gilchrist opined heavily, ignoring her husband's instant vocal denial of such a possibility. 'It's the *only* possible explanation for this. Nobody else would have known where to find those photos or had access to them.'

'Why the devil would Jason launch a vicious character assassination on his sister on the very day of her wedding?' Gerald Gilchrist demanded.

'Because he's very bitter and selling a sleazy story like that would have got him a lot of money,' Ella's mother breathed in a pained undertone. 'Of course, he told a lot of lies to spice it up—it probably got him a bigger pay-out.'

'Let's not judge without proof,' her father urged uneasily.

'How much proof do you need, Gerald? He's moved out into a flat we didn't know he owned and he texted you to tell you he'd gone skiing yesterday.' Jennifer Gilchrist sighed. 'Where did he get the money to pay for an expensive holiday when he told us he was broke?'

In growing dismay, Ella was studying a more colourful image of herself, racily dressed in a short black leather skirt and a low-necked lace top with fake black wings attached. It had been taken at a Halloween fancy-dress party the previous year. Cathy by her side, the two girls were giggling and slightly the worse for wear. As well as a large photo of Zarif looking very forbidding there was one of a man she didn't recognise and that snapshot was labelled 'Ex-boyfriend, Matt Barton'. Who on earth was Matt Barton? Ella finally took in the headline: THE SEX EXPLOITS OF A FUTURE QUEEN.

Exploits? *What exploits?* Her tummy executing a sick somersault, Ella thrust back a chair and began to read. The salacious content of the article sent shock reeling through her in waves. This Matt Barton claimed she had attended sex parties with him and he called her 'an adventurous woman with a voracious appetite for sex and new experiences.' She was gobsmacked.

'Is it *all* lies?' her father queried darkly. 'I mean, who's this Matt Barton chap? Why have we never heard of him before?'

'Probably because I've never heard of him either…in fact I've never seen him before and I've certainly never gone out with him,' Ella declared between compressed lips as she read. 'Apparently he owns some London nightclub that's just closed down…I do hope Zarif doesn't take this newspaper,' she concluded weakly.

But that was a hope destined to end in instant disappointment when a large dark man in a suit knocked loudly on the back door for entry. As her father lurched forward to deal angrily with what he assumed to be another reporter Ella glanced out, only to be totally transfixed by the sight of Zarif poised squarely in the middle of their large back lawn, clearly having used the back entrance to avoid the photographers on the doorstep. 'It's Zarif,' she framed warningly.

'Oh, well, the more the merrier…but the bridegroom is not supposed to see the bride before the wedding.' Her mother twittered in consternation while she unlocked the back door.

Five men as big and bulky as army tanks and clearly bodyguards ringed Zarif. Immaculate in an exquisitely tailored grey pinstripe suit cut to enhance every line of his tall, broad-shouldered, lean-hipped body, he settled grim dark golden eyes on her. He still looked unutterably gorgeous. She had realised that his mood made little impression on his heartbreaking good looks the day he first proposed and stood there silently seething at her rejection without losing a single ounce of his charismatic attraction. He stalked into the kitchen, uttering a strained but polite acknowledgement of her parents' presence while her father noisily bundled up the offending newspaper and thrust it into the bin. His real attention, however, was locked to Ella.

Ella reddened, caught barefoot in her comfy tartan pyjamas and ancient fleece dressing gown without a scrap of make-up to hide behind. Damn him for not phoning first, she thought initially, because though the landline might be off the hook he had her cell number and he had chosen not to make use of it. Had he deliberately chosen that element of surprise? *Sex parties?* After reading that ludicrous claim, Ella was convinced that nothing in life would ever surprise her again. She had not the slightest doubt that Zarif had read the same newspaper. Was he now planning to call off the wedding? Consternation filled her, teaching her that, without even knowing it, she had become accustomed to the idea of becoming his wife.

'Ella…may we talk?' Zarif breathed grittily, running eyes as bright as polished black jet over her somewhat bedraggled appearance. Her golden mane fell untidily round her shoulders, framing the luminous oval of her face and somehow magically highlighting her beautiful eyes.

Sex parties, he thought with a rage beyond anything he had ever experienced—a rage that was only held in restraint by a lifetime of iron discipline. The very thought of other men seeing her naked, not to mention the image of her lying beneath another man, sent an energising charge of pure violence roaring through Zarif's tall powerful frame. He wanted to beat someone up, shoot something, smash his fists into walls and shed blood. The idea that there could have been a whole legion of men already well acquainted with the leggy perfection of her slender, curvaceous body sent Zarif into a towering rage.

Ella rose from her seat and led the way into the little-used dining room, turning only when she reached the head of the table to look back at him, her chin set at a mutinous angle as he thrust the door firmly shut behind him. He was going to do it; she knew he was going to do it. He *was* going to ask the one unforgivable question.

Zarif released his breath on a slow hiss. 'Is it true?'

There he was, bang on target, she thought crazily, almost drunk with the sudden rush of anger and disappointment that he could, for even one moment, credit such wild and fantastic stories about her. 'Which bit? The insatiable desire for sex and the latest kink? Or the sex parties?' she questioned tightly. 'Choose your answer… it's all the same to me.'

Taken aback by her boldness, Zarif shot her an incredulous appraisal, his strong jawline hardening. 'Don't take that attitude with me. I have the right to ask.'

'No, you don't have any rights over me. I'm not married to you yet. You didn't question my past when you had the opportunity and I didn't question you about *yours* either… It's a little late in the day to start changing your mind now.'

His ridiculously long black lashes screened his gaze and a dark flush rose to accentuate the exotic line of his high cheekbones. Something she had said had really hit home hard with him but unfortunately she didn't know which part of her brave speech had struck him like an arrow hitting a bullseye. Indeed she only grasped that she had, for once, inexplicably achieved the feat of putting Zarif out of countenance.

'Unhappily I do not have the freedom to overlook a wife's colourful past. I have too many
other considerations to take into account, not
least the royal status I would be granting you,'
Zarif bit out, lean tanned hands clenching into
fists by his side. He could give her up; of course
he could give her up if he had to. He could re-
visit the idea of putting her in the Dubai apartment though, couldn't he? The choking tightness
banding his chest receded just a little, comforted
by that reflection.

What was she playing at? What the heck was
she playing at? Ella asked herself in sudden disconcertion because with a few defiant, well-
chosen words she could easily blow her parents'
rescue plan right out of the water and she had no
wish to do that. But Zarif had disappointed her
expectations, demeaning and offending her by
asking her that inexcusable question.

Is it true?

But she could see his point; she could *really* see
and understand his point. Vashir was a conservative country and a scandal-besmirched queen
would be about as welcome there as snow in the

desert. Jason had played a blinder, she thought painfully, for how could she possibly defend herself against such accusations? Didn't mud always cling to such victims? But, hell roast it, she was nobody's victim and certainly not her greedy brother's!

'Surely you had my lifestyle checked out before you proposed?' Ella prompted, because it would have struck her as incredibly reckless of him to have proposed without first assuring himself of her continuing suitability and she refused to believe that Zarif had a single reckless bone in his body. 'Surely you already know the answer to your own question?'

'Regrettably not. I had no thought of marriage in mind when we met at the hotel,' Zarif admitted stonily, furious that she wasn't giving him a straight answer.

'My goodness, that was very irresponsible and quite unlike you,' Ella told him in dulcet surprise, her golden head tilting to one side as if she was taking special note of that fact.

His dark-as-molasses eyes flamed tawny gold, his outrage at her mockery unconcealed. *'Answer me!'* he instructed her rawly, his tone cracking like a whip in the smouldering silence.

'Exactly what sort of a past did you think I might have?' Ella enquired in a brittle voice, striving not to yield an inch at the intimidating mien of granite-hard purpose and authority that had hardened his darkly handsome face. He could be tough but she could be tough too when it came to self-defence.

'Nothing out of the ordinary. Obviously I'm not expecting you to be a virgin. I assume you've had the usual adult experiences and I have no desire to pry any more intimately than that into your past. But *that*,' Zarif breathed with harsh emphasis, 'would be my personal outlook. In my public role I have to take into account my people and what they expect from their royal family. We are an old-fashioned people and my family is expected to set high standards. I would also like to know how all this got into the hands of the press.'

'Family photos appeared in that article… Mum and I think that Jason sold the story.'

Zarif frowned in disbelief. '*Jason* has done this to you?'

'You seem surprised. But Jason is burning with resentment and bitterness right now. He's not going to profit in any way from our marriage and that has enraged him.'

'I had assumed he would take the benefits to your parents into account.'

Ella rolled her eyes at that principled view. 'My brother has a vengeful streak. Since you're cut from the same cloth, you should understand that.'

Fresh outrage roared through Zarif. 'In no way can you compare me to your brother!'

'Blackmailing me into marrying you to get me into bed is revenge,' Ella informed him shortly. 'Maybe you still think it's a big thrill and an honour for me but I don't feel the same way.'

'You still haven't answered my question about the veracity of that newspaper story,' Zarif reminded her with stubborn grit, furious that she had labelled his generosity as blackmail when he saw it as something else entirely.

'Because…really, you don't deserve an answer,' Ella condemned with an angry bitterness she couldn't hide. 'And you should be ashamed that you even asked. You knew me three years ago. Can you really credit that I've changed that much?'

A forbidding edge hardened Zarif's jawline. 'I have lived long enough to accept that people *do* change in unexpected ways. Events can make people act out of character,' he pointed out flatly, refusing to yield an inch on that score for he himself had once behaved in such a way.

'I bow to your superior knowledge, but choosing not to marry you three years ago didn't push me into trying out the lifestyle of a porn queen,' Ella declared with licking scorn, blue eyes mutinously bright. 'I've never heard of Matt Barton before, never even met him. I suspect he's someone Jason paid to malign me as, being my brother, it would be odd for Jason to have made sexual allegations against me and it would also have meant exposing the fact that he sold me down the river in the first place.'

A small tithe of the tension holding Zarif rigid eased. 'You've never even met the man who is referred to as your ex-boyfriend?' he pressed.

'You're saying the whole story is a lie? Don't tell me that just to impress me because I will investigate this matter further.'

'Right at this moment,' Ella proclaimed, tossing back her head so that rumpled golden hair tumbled in glossy disarray round her shoulders, 'I haven't the *smallest* desire to impress you.'

'But you *do* need to ensure that our wedding goes ahead,' Zarif reminded her in a roughened undertone because he was noticing that the well-washed cotton of her pyjama jacket was snagging on her pointed nipples, vaguely delineating the firm, full curves of the breasts he longed to explore. He swallowed back a curse, infuriated by his loss of focus and the suspicion that he was behaving like a sex-starved teenage boy.

Zarif's reminder was unnecessary because Ella was painfully aware that her parents' future security was reliant on what she did next. He had gravely offended her but he was the one in the position of power, not she, and, while she refused to grovel, she also saw that she had to fully defend herself to clear her name. 'I'm telling you the truth. I'm not guilty of any of it. I would never *go* to a sex party. I've been set up for a fall and horribly slandered in newsprint.'

'If you are certain that this is the case, I will sue,' Zarif asserted, dark golden eyes welded to her flushed and indignant face with satisfaction. 'But be warned, if I do sue any intimate secrets you have in that line will inevitably be exposed by the proceedings.'

'I have no such secrets,' Ella parried curtly, sucking in a deep sustaining breath. 'My conscience is clean as a whistle. You go ahead and sue.'

'Should I be prepared for genuine disclosures to emerge from any of your former lovers?' Zarif enquired between visibly gritted teeth.

CHAPTER FOUR

ELLA'S EYES GLINTED. Of course she could have told Zarif the truth that she had yet to have a lover but he didn't *deserve* that revelation. Her eyelids lowered secretively while a smile that was amused, but came across as saucy, unexpectedly curved her lips. 'No. In that line you're safe. I've always been cautious about who I choose to date.'

Zarif's gaze burned gold when he saw that smile because he was convinced that she was fondly recalling one of her lovers. He breathed in slow and deep. He was not the jealous, possessive type—what was the matter with him? Other men had slept with her, discovered the secrets of that slim, curvaceous body, listened to her cries of pleasure… Get over it, he told himself impatiently, fighting the tide of destructive X-rated imagery threatening to engulf him. 'This has been a most unlucky start to our wedding day.'

'Yes—' Ella shrugged a careless shoulder '—but let's not pretend it's a real wedding day or that we're people who care about each other like a normal bride and groom.'

His nostrils flared. 'I can assure you that it will be a *real* wedding and that I *do* care about your well-being.'

'Not convinced...sorry about that.' Beneath his disconcerted gaze, Ella lifted a slender hand and screened an uninterested yawn in a disdainful gesture as she moved towards him, keen to show him out of the house. 'If you'd cared, you would have offered me support and felt angry on my behalf.'

Even less accustomed to censure than he was to scorn, Zarif squared his sculpted jaw. 'That is unjust. How would I know whether it was the truth or not when I haven't had any contact with you for years?'

Unimpressed, Ella raised a delicate honey-coloured brow. 'Do you think you could leave now so that I can have breakfast and go do the bridal stuff?' she asked sweetly.

Zarif shot out a lean brown hand and closed it

round her wrist to stop her in her tracks. 'You will not speak to me like that or try to dismiss me like a servant,' he told her angrily.

'Does that really matter as long as I go to bed with you?' Ella asked in a brittle voice. 'Do you honestly also expect me to be servile like some sort of medieval sex slave?'

Zarif glowered down at her in seething frustration. She was being childish, her immaturity spelt out in cheap gibes and he was tempted to shake her. *'Stop it.'*

He towered over her, so close that she could smell the faint spicy tang of designer cologne that was achingly familiar to her. Suddenly tears stung the backs of her eyelids as a tide of almost forgotten memories threatened to drown her: deceptively romantic moments three years earlier when he had held her hand, given her thoughtful little gifts, listened carefully to her concerns, acted in a way that was protective and caring. And *it had all been a lie*, she reminded herself bitterly, because his true feelings for her had gone no deeper than a lusty desire to take her to bed and ensure that she became conveniently pregnant with the required son and heir.

'Eleonora…' Zarif chided huskily, running his finger down her cheek to trace the path of an escaped tear. 'You're upset, angry.'

Ella looked up at him, involuntarily enthralled by the beauty of his dark fallen-angel features, the sheer richness of his stunning amber-gold gaze framed by luxuriant ebony lashes. She shivered, inordinately aware of the brush of his finger across her cheek. 'Don't—'

'I *must*,' Zarif growled hoarsely, his hand dropping to her chin to push it up to enable his mouth to come down with hungry driving dominance on hers. Taken by surprise, Ella reeled dizzily, mouth opening to receive the erotic plunge of his tongue. He tasted so wonderfully good, a knot tightened in her pelvis and she gasped, feeling the scandalous dampness of desire surge between her taut thighs in treacherous contrast to her anger with him. The comparison shocked her and broke through the mesmeric power of his mouth on hers.

'No, don't,' Ella protested, squirming against

his lean, powerful frame in a manner that only stretched his control thinner than ever.

'Tonight you'll be mine,' Zarif pronounced with unashamed satisfaction, lifting her up against him as though she were a doll and planting her on the edge of the table, pushing her knees apart to stand between them, leaning forward to thrust his aroused body into the apex of her thighs.

Tingling awareness bubbled like a volcano low in her body. Her bright blue eyes widened, pupils dilated as she stared back at him because for once they were on a level. He had sinfully sexy eyes. Her top felt scratchy and uncomfortable against her tender breasts and her breath was catching in her throat. A voice was screaming in the back of her mind, telling her to get a grip, but what kept her still was the warm liquid melting sensation steadily spreading through her lower limbs and most pressing of all, at its pinnacle, a downright unbearable physical ache for the fulfilment she had never known. 'And you'll love every moment of what I do to you,' Zarif forecast hoarsely.

Ella heard his voice through the wall of sensation caused by the outrageous stroke of the long, lean fingers encircling her hips just below her top, the touch of his fingertips across her skin alerting her to an innate sensuality she had not had the chance to experience with him before. She could feel his erection through the fine barrier of his pants and the knowledge that she aroused him even in her pjs and without make-up was ridiculously empowering. She struggled to draw another breath past her tight throat as he pressed his mouth hungrily against the tender skin between her neck and her shoulder and her head fell back without her volition, a tiny gasp escaping her parted lips.

His hands slid up beneath her top and cupped the full globes of her breasts and excitement sent her heart racing so fast she felt light-headed. The surge of heat and wetness between her thighs as he tugged at her straining nipples sent shock-waves through her as his mouth found hers again with a raw passion that thrilled her. Her hands clutched at his arms, nails biting into his sleeves, frustration hurtling through her that she couldn't touch him the way he was touching her.

'Oh, I'm so sorry…!' The sound of her mother's

voice and the door opening and closing again in fast succession roused Ella from her sexual stupor as nothing else could have done. She opened her eyes, not even recalling when she had closed them.

Infuriatingly, Zarif had regained control first and had already stepped back from her. She clashed with burning golden eyes and snatched in a shuddering breath, her face crimson as she acknowledged what she had allowed to happen between them. And when she was furious with him too? That was the most galling admission of all: that Zarif could touch her and every other consideration could simply melt away.

'I will see you later, *habibti*,' Zarif murmured tautly, a flush lining his hard cheekbones.

Ella slid off the table like an electrified eel and hauled open the door. Her mother beamed at her from the hall. 'The beautician's here and you haven't had breakfast yet,' she fussed. 'Will Zarif be staying?'

'No...' From behind her, Zarif took over the conversation with effortless ease and not the smallest hint of discomfiture.

* * *

Zarif watched his bride exchanging greetings with the children of some of the guests. She was good with little ones, he recognised, watching her animated face and her sparkling eyes as she laughed and chatted, displaying the first warmth she had shown since he saw her at the church. She was so naturally beautiful in her simple elegant gown he had found it a challenge to look away. She had played the bridal role with a shuttered look in her gaze though, polite and smiling but with all true feeling edited out of the show. *His* wife. The designation still felt like a shock—almost as much of a shock as it had been to his uncle Halim when he phoned him three weeks earlier to break the news.

'Of course, it is past time for you to take a wife,' Halim has declared valiantly, holding back on the word, '*again*', diplomatic and generous to the end. 'And British like your grandmother? She will be a popular choice with those who wish us to look West rather than East as we move into the future. I shall look forward to meeting her.'

And for an instant Zarif had felt a piercing shame that he was about to foist such a sham on the old man, who had watched his only child, Azel, become Zarif's first wife, queen and mother before the heart-rending car crash took both her life and that of their son. Devastated, Halim had taken refuge in his academic books, finally requesting permission to leave palace politics and return to his professorship at the university where lectures and students had, at least, distracted him from his grief.

Times without number, Zarif had crushed the futile wish that he too could find such an outlet to escape his memories because the only change in his daily life had been a constant shadow of indescribable loss. Even so, Zarif was well aware that his remarriage, his doing what *had* to be done and before Halim died, would be a comfort to the older man. After all, Halim had raised his nephew to believe that the stability of Vashir came first and last, before personal feelings, *before* everything else. And now, for the first time in his life, Zarif was suddenly shockingly conscious that he was guilty of betraying his duty because he had allowed his desire to possess Ella Gilchrist to suppress every other consideration.

Across the room, a little girl was examining Ella's shiny new platinum wedding band and complaining mournfully that it didn't sparkle and Ella was explaining the difference between wedding and engagement rings, a clarification that ran out of steam when she was asked why *she* didn't have an engagement ring.

Rising to her feet with a rather stilted laugh, Ella abandoned the challenge, her attention roaming to Zarif, tall, dark and extraordinarily handsome in a tailored morning suit teamed with a grey striped silk cravat, where he was chatting to her parents. He was so damned smooth and polished in his every move that she wanted to scream. Nobody would ever have guessed that the wedding was a charade that cast a respectable veil over the most basic transaction possible between a man and a woman. Inside herself she shrank, thinking there could be little difference between her and any other woman who sold her body for money, for wasn't that exactly what she was doing?

And worst of all, with a male who felt absolutely nothing for her, she reflected wretchedly, for while Zarif's outer façade of cool might have convinced their small select band of guests that he was a joyful bridegroom, it had not fooled Ella. That rare flashing smile of his had not been in evidence once. She just *knew* he was thinking about Azel because she could feel the distance and reserve in him, see the haunting darkness in his eyes. The one and only time he had discussed his first wife with her had been the day he proposed marriage to Ella three years earlier and his words then were still branded into her soul like unhealed wounds.

He had referred to Azel as *irreplaceable* while assuring Ella that he was not asking her to supplant his first wife in her role as that would, apparently, have been an impossible task.

And when she had asked Zarif if he loved her in surely the most poignant question a young woman in love could ask?

'I will always hold Azel in my heart. I cannot pretend otherwise.'

And yet after that little speech, the living proof

that some men wouldn't understand or recognise emotion unless it was tipped over their heads like boiling oil, Zarif had been stunned when Ella turned his proposal down. Even madly in love and at only twenty-one years of age, Ella had foreseen what a disaster it would have been for her to have even *tried* to follow in Azel's perfect footsteps. Zarif, whether he had known it or not, hadn't been ready or able to put another woman in Azel's place. Ella, heartbroken, had backed off from such an impossible and thankless challenge.

Accordingly, there Zarif was now mere hours after marrying Ella, no doubt looking back with regret to his first wedding day when he had had the joy of wedding a woman he loved with all his heart and his soul. The very thought hurt, just as it had hurt like an acid burn all those years ago when Ella had been forced to accept that, although she adored Zarif and longed for him with every cell in her body, he would have sacrificed her in a moment if, by some miracle, he could have brought Azel back to life.

He wouldn't have wanted Azel purely for sex,

Ella acknowledged unhappily. He had loved and respected Azel and Ella was challenged to understand what she herself had done to rouse such hostility in Zarif that would incur such a devastating revenge. Three years ago, she had said no and her excuses had gone down like a brick on glass but even though she had been in an agony of pain at his virtual rejection of her she had certainly not intended to cause offence.

Of course, rejection had to have been something entirely new to Zarif, she acknowledged ruefully. All women noticed his stunning dark good looks, automatically turning to take a second glance when he was nearby. Those brief weeks she had dated him it had been like going out with a movie star, for everywhere they went women had watched, giggled flirtatiously and tried to catch his eye. He had seemed sublimely unconscious of the effect he had on her sex. He seemed not to have an ounce of vanity but how reliable a character witness was she?

After all, it would never have occurred to Ella three years ago that Zarif would sink to the level of literally *paying* her to share his bed. As soon as she thought that, Ella frowned, reminding herself that she had agreed to his terms for the sake of the parents she loved. *Her* choice, then, and even if she couldn't quite manage to be grateful that he had given her that choice, she knew it would be unjust to blame Zarif for how she felt now that she had accepted the role of mistress within marriage from him. Unhappily, the 'sex and nothing but sex' label made her feel worthless and degraded.

There could be no denying that Zarif had changed and much more than she could ever have expected. The man she remembered had been so upright and so straight in every way and it was ironic that only now when she no longer loved him was she learning that he had a much darker, more complex side to his character and that could only make her fear for her future.

Ella stared wide-eyed at the opulence of the private jet with its cream leather sofas and luxurious fittings, not to mention the four uniformed cabin staff bowing and scraping respectfully in their presence. She finally sat down, nerves bubbling in her tummy at the knowledge that once the craft was airborne she was leaving home and everything familiar behind. Who knew when she might return?

Already it felt as if the day, which had begun with such drama, was turning into the longest day in existence. They were flying to Vashir and tomorrow would undergo a second wedding ceremony in the presence of Zarif's ailing uncle Halim and the local VIPs. Just then it felt as if she were facing another endurance test in how to please everyone other than herself.

Zarif studied his bride with barely repressed hunger burning in his veiled gaze. Her delicate profile was as taut as her slender body and his attention lingered on the flutter of her lashes, the slim, elegant hand resting on her lap and, more potently, on the thrust of the luscious breasts he had stroked. The hem of her royal-blue dress exposed long shapely legs and he breathed in slow and deep, disturbed by the force of desire gripping him and unaccustomed to such a challenge to his self-control.

No other woman did this to him. He didn't

know what it was about Ella but he had barely to look at her to get hard and he shifted in his seat because the tight heaviness at his groin was uncomfortable. Temptation lurked in the existence of the sleeping compartment at the back of the main cabin but it was cramped and time would be short. He didn't want a quick snack, he wanted a feast, a consummation worthy of the time he had waited for her. *His*, *at last*, he savoured, in name if not yet in action.

Ella leafed through a glossy fashion magazine with blank eyes, her tension rising in the silence rather than abating. 'I was surprised your brothers weren't on the guest list today,' she said abruptly.

'They will be attending our wedding tomorrow,' Zarif proffered. 'I imagine you will be glad of Betsy and Belle's company.'

'I hardly know them, but I suppose so,' Ella conceded in such a limp voice that Zarif wanted to shake her.

Anyone could be forgiven for thinking that marrying him and becoming a queen was a cruel and unusual punishment, Zarif reflected in exasperation. Of course, it was only for a year, he recalled absently, wondering why he hadn't demanded two years or even three until he remembered that sooner rather than later he had to marry for real and reproduce and he marvelled that he could even have momentarily forgotten that salient fact.

'Why didn't you tell me that your mother had had a heart attack and your father a breakdown?' Zarif demanded without warning. 'Your father's friend, Jonathan, spoke to me at the reception and clearly assumed that I already knew.'

Ella compressed her lips. 'I didn't think that plucking a thousand violin strings would cut any ice with you.'

'Telling me would not have been plucking strings,' Zarif censured. 'It would have been giving me relevant facts and it would have changed my outlook.'

Ella shot him a dark look. 'I doubt that very much. I didn't sense any compassion in the room.'

Zarif gritted his teeth, exasperated that she could think him that cruel. Her parents were good, decent people, who had been kind and welcoming to him for several years without any hope of reward or profit. 'You have a seven-hour flight during which I expect you to get over your sulk and accept your new status,' he delivered grimly once the jet was in the air.

'I do *not* sulk!' Ella exclaimed furiously, her blonde head swivelling to deal a fiery glance at his lean, dark, beautiful face.

'Oh, I can assure you that you do,' Zarif drawled, smooth as glass. 'But I am impervious to such moods.'

Ella undid her seat-belt fastening and shot upright as though jet-propelled. 'I will say it once more only...*I am not in a mood!*' She launched the declaration furiously down at him. 'You're as insensitive as a rock. Have you no concept of how difficult it is for me to leave my home to live in a foreign country with a different culture and a man who doesn't even have the saving grace of loving me? Have you any idea how I felt today *lying* and putting on a fake happy-bride act for all my family and friends?'

Zarif stayed where he was and contemplated her with an immense sense of satisfaction for the Ella he knew best was back on display. Her volatile emotions and innate spirit never failed to entertain him while other women displaying similar tendencies had swiftly been dismissed from his life, he acknowledged dimly. But in a rage, Ella was magnificent, sapphire-blue eyes splintering defiance, lovely face angrily flushed, lush bee-stung lips prominent and offering pure pink invitation.

'Are you just going to sit there saying nothing?' Ella positively snarled, nonplussed by his stillness and lack of reaction.

'When you get all steamed up,' Zarif murmured huskily, 'you look incredibly hot and sexy.'

Ella did what any sane woman would have done, because it was clear that he had not paid heed to a single word she had said. She lifted her glass of water and emptied it over his arrogant dark head. 'Then it's time you cooled off...'

Totally taken aback by that liquid assault, Zarif sprang upright, tawny eyes ablaze with anger and no small amount of disbelief as he flicked dripping black hair off his wide, intelligent brow. 'You are behaving like a madwoman!'

'No, a madwoman would have used a knife, not water,' Ella told him succinctly. 'Now I will say it again. I was not sulking. I'm simply nervous about the challenge of embracing a new lifestyle.'

'And so you should be because I am no push-over when I lose my temper!' Zarif grated as he snatched her off her feet without the smallest warning and stalked stormily down the cabin to thrust open the door at the foot.

'Put me down!' Ella yelled at him.

Zarif dropped her from a height down onto a bed without a great deal of bounce and she fell back against the pillows, bright honey-coloured hair rioting round her flushed features. She surveyed him in shock as he began to wrench off his jacket and haul at his tie. 'What are you doing?' she demanded.

'You soaked my clothing,' he reminded her grittily as he ripped open the buttons on the white silk shirt plastered to his muscular chest. 'And if we're about to have a row, we will stage it in here where it is more private.'

Ella sat up, more than a little embarrassed at the water she had thrown over him. 'I shouldn't have drenched you...but when you go all stony-faced and unemotional, I *hate* it!'

'I *am* unemotional by nature,' Zarif shot back at her as he stripped off the shirt. 'I'm afraid you'll just have to learn to deal with that. Assaulting me isn't an option I'm prepared to tolerate.'

Ella's tummy somersaulted and a slow heavy heat spread in her pelvis as she looked at him because he, undoubtedly, had the most beautiful male body she had ever seen. Roped muscle defined his broad bronzed torso. Dark whorls of hair adorned his impressive pecs, arrowing down over a flat washboard stomach to disappear below the belt encircling his lean hips. For a split second, he simply took her breath away.

'Particularly when there are so many more entertaining possibilities on offer now,' Zarif completed softly as he came down on his knees on the bed beside her, still bare chested, his tailored trousers pulling taut across his lean, powerful thighs.

Unnerved, Ella froze like a stone pillar. 'I don't know what you mean.'

'Of course you do,' Zarif contradicted, running

a mocking fingertip along the compressed line of her mouth. 'Freezing into stillness like an animal being hunted isn't going to save you. You're my wife. I can touch you, *hunt* you any time I like...'

That awareness had taunted Ella from the moment he whipped off his shirt without a shade of self-consciousness to expose his glowing bronzed skin and whipcord muscles. But then why would Zarif be self-conscious in any intimate situation? Ella mocked her own naivety, all too painfully aware of the many highly experienced lovers he had evidently enjoyed. He was so close now that she could have reached out and touched him and her fingers braced harder to the mattress as if she feared being tempted. And she *did* fear it because he had always tempted her and it would destroy her self-respect if she gave him anything more than passive compliance.

Zarif lowered his head and used his lips to pluck teasingly at the taut line of hers. Oxygen feathered in her tight throat and with a faint gasp she opened her mouth. But he continued to play games with her, suckling at her lower lip and then darting the tip of his tongue along the underside of her lip, setting off an astonishing flurry of reaction that slithered through her like a sweet piercing dart that went deep. She trembled, astonishingly aware of the prickling tightness of her nipples, and then all of a sudden, literally between one breath and the next, she wanted his mouth hard on hers with a ferocity that shook her. Her hands wanted to claw into his hair to drag his head down to hers.

Her head fell back on her shoulders even as she felt the faint brush of his fingers against her spine. Cooler air washed her backbone and surprise gripped her as she registered that he had unzipped her dress without her even noticing. Her lashes flew up, her gaze connecting with scorching gold fringed with lush black lashes. He had such beautiful eyes, she acknowledged, and every other thought in her head evaporated simultaneously.

Zarif tugged the perfumed weight of her honey-blonde hair forward as he eased the dress down her arms. 'I always loved your hair... It's the most amazing colour when the sun catches it.'

'No sun here,' she framed nervously, feeling

alarmingly shy at being stripped down to her bra and panties. He was coolly undressing her without a hint of passion and she was so unnerved by the experience that she could not even contemplate the much greater intimacy that surely still lay ahead of her.

Hard as a rock, Zarif studied the ripe mounds of her full breasts and swiftly removed the bra to cup the lush heavy globes in his appreciative hands. He stroked the quivering tips to aching sensitivity and only then did he kiss her.

Ella quivered, her whole body alight and tingling. Her hands dug into his shoulders as he took her rosy nipples between his fingers while claiming her mouth in a long drugging kiss. He skated his tongue across the sensitive roof of her mouth and she gasped, starting to moan as he let his tongue plunge deep in a much more primitive demand. The ache in her pelvis tightened like a knot being snapped tight, every atom of control wrested from her as mindless hunger took her in a shocking surge.

Zarif tugged her down flat on the bed, deft hands releasing her from the confines of the dress creased round her hips. He kept on kissing her and, oh, he was *so* good at it that she was on fire, pushing closer to his lean, hard body, wanting more, her entire body stimulated to a painful degree by responses more powerful than any she had previously experienced.

Zarif lifted his head to gaze down at her while he trailed his fingers through the damp tangle of curls at the apex of her thighs. 'I want to watch you writhe and come, *habibti*,' he husked. 'I want to hear you scream with the pleasure I give you.'

'Don't want to scream,' Ella framed with the greatest of difficulty, so hard was it for her to control her breathing and her voice enough to speak.

A fingertip found the swollen bud of her clitoris and dallied. He knew exactly what he was doing. He touched and she burned with every delicate caress. Her hips rose off the mattress in a movement as old and unstoppable as time. She struggled to breathe, actually sobbed out loud as he lowered his proud dark head and captured an engorged pink nipple between his lips and teased with his teeth. As he divided his attention between her straining, unbearably sensitive breasts and the tormentingly tender bud between her thighs, the twin assault became too much for her to bear. The hollow sensation at the heart of her was getting stronger while rhythmic waves were washing through her womb until suddenly the knot of tension there sprang free, plunging her into the grip of writhing convulsions of almost intolerable pleasure.

That shattering climax and the flood of ecstasy that followed took her by storm.

Zarif stared down at her, glittering tawny eyes alight with a new knowledge that made Ella cringe. She closed her eyes in self-protection, shamed by her complete loss of control. He pulled a sheet over her.

'Get some rest,' he advised smoothly. 'Tomorrow's festivities will last even longer than today's and tonight I would prefer you wide awake.'

Hot with mortification and with her body still liquid as melting honey from his sensual attentions, Ella lay there long after the cabin door had closed behind him. It was only Zarif she could not resist, she tried to tell herself in consolation.

Other men had tried and failed to seduce her into going further than she wanted to but Zarif did not even have to try. Why was that? How would she ever look him in the face again? At least, however, he would know what he was doing even she did not, she told herself soothingly, nervous tension pinching at her as she considered the night that still lay ahead.

CHAPTER FIVE

THE AIRPORT LAY just outside the city of Qurzah. The jet landed to be greeted by a formal welcome in the form of a military band, a crowd of officials and a very cute little girl in a fancy frock, who curtsied and presented Ella with a bouquet. Ella was relieved that she had followed her mother's advice and chosen a classy outfit to travel in because her mostly vintage wardrobe would not have met conservative expectations. Her blue shift dress, jacket and high heels, however, exactly fitted the bill.

Zarif watched his bride respond with beaming charm to the greetings and would have been more impressed had she once aimed those sparkling eyes and smiles in his direction. She was stubborn, capricious and paraded her moods too easily.

He marvelled that he had asked her to marry

him *for real* only three years earlier. What *had* he been thinking of? Had he become obsessed by his overwhelming desire to make her his? Unlike him she had not been raised to respect the concept of duty or the rules and the restraint that went hand in hand with the exalted and privileged status of the al-Rastani dynasty. When the time came, he would be practical and he would seek a wife from one of the other Gulf royal families, one who knew exactly what he needed from her, he reflected grimly, wondering why the very prospect of that day should make his heart sink like a stone.

The limo wafted them through the crowded streets of Qurzah and he watched Ella look surprised when she saw the modern layout of the city as well as the shopping malls and the many parks adorned with fountains and sculptures. 'It's just like any city,' she remarked in evident relief. 'But rather more attractive than many I've visited.'

'We are not a backward or primitive country,' Zarif countered drily. 'The oil wealth of decades and an education system and health service second to none have naturally made their mark.'

'I didn't think Vashir was backward...although you don't let women drive here,' Ella commented in a small aside redolent of her incredulity at such an embargo.

Zarif breathed in deep and slow and tried not to grit his teeth. He sometimes thought that his country was more famous for that restriction than for anything else and he would be changing that perverse law as soon as his uncle was no more. To do so beforehand had struck him as needlessly distressing for the old man, rousing as it would grievous memories that were better left buried.

The limo purred between lofty gates into a property surrounded by tall walls and turrets. Ella gazed in wonderment at the vast ancient building stretched out before her because with its Moorish arches, weathered and elaborate stonework and the glorious greenery softening the frontage it was very redolent of an Arabian nights fantasy dwelling. 'I thought the palace was brand new.'

'The new one is on the other side of the city and used for government council meetings, conferences and all official functions. This is where I grew up and I prefer to live here, certainly while my uncle is ill,' Zarif proffered, his beautiful wilful mouth tightening as if he was waiting for her to argue.

Ella said nothing although she had pinned her confidence on staying at the new palace where she could be secure in the awareness that Zarif's first wife could never have lived there. So much for that hope! And why should she be so oversensitive anyway? It was not as if she were in love with Zarif or jealous, she reasoned, exasperated by her odd thought train.

She slid from the car. Darkness was falling and the heat was already less oppressive than it had been at the airport where within minutes of being deprived of air-conditioning cool her dress had literally felt as though it were plastered to her damp, perspiring skin. 'It looks like a fascinating building.'

'Hamid will show you round.' Zarif referred to his chief aide. 'His father used to be in charge of running the old palace and he, too, grew up here. He knows everything about the palace's history.'

Ella would have been more impressed had Zarif offered to conduct such a tour personally and kept her expressive eyes veiled as she reasoned that she had been shown her true importance in the grand scheme of things again. Not that she wasn't already well aware of her lowly status. Regardless of the fleeting intimacy they had shared, Zarif remained ultra-cool and detached. Her body might still hum at the very thought of his fingers trailing across her sensitive skin but he was still as remote as the Andes.

A small crowd of women in distinctly elaborate clothing waited two steps inside the giant front doors of an echoing stone hall ornamented by a long parade of pillars.

'I am Hanya,' a very pretty dark-eyed brunette informed Ella in perfect English. 'I will look after you until tomorrow.'

Zarif froze on the threshold, ebony brows pleating and rising in a frown. 'Where are you taking my wife, Hanya?' he demanded abruptly.

'According to the imam Miss Ella Gilchrist will not be your legal wife or our queen until tomorrow, cousin,' Hanya announced in a soft, deeply apologetic tone, her head bowing low as if she hated to break such news. 'Our uncle discussed his regard for the old ways with me and I'm afraid this is what he expects.'

Zarif almost looked heavenward to pray for patience but restrained the urge. Hanya had been cousin to Azel and insisted on maintaining the bond between them created by marriage. But Hanya was right. Halim was an old-fashioned man, always eager to venerate the proprieties. Clearly, Zarif had another day to wait before he was able to claim his bride. He threw back his shoulders, ready to lay down the law and refuse to part with her to a separate bed. After all, Ella was still his wife even if she hadn't yet married him according to Vashiri law and the concept of restraining his already very unruly libido for still longer had no appeal whatsoever.

A year, his more honourable and tolerant self reminded him staunchly, to take the edge off his temper. Ella would be his for an entire year… surely he could wait another day? He did not want to disappoint or alarm his uncle and with a brief jerk of his arrogant dark head he strode past, pausing only to say to Ella, 'I will see you tomorrow, then.'

'Thank you, Your Majesty.' Hanya, who had an extremely irritating laugh, giggled like a little girl and clutched Ella's sleeve with a dainty, perfectly manicured hand. 'I will show you to your suite...come this way.'

The following morning Ella winced and cringed through what had amounted to a public bathing experience in which she was surrounded by a flock of strange women wanting to bath her, wax her and anoint her body and her hair with exotic scented oils. After that ordeal, being wrapped in a modern towelling robe felt refreshingly normal, and it was almost relaxing to have to sit down and patiently wait while a pair of henna artists knelt on the floor beside her to draw intricate swirling patterns onto her hands and her feet.

Indeed Ella was feeling remarkably tolerant and relieved that she was getting through the trial of the wedding preparations without losing her temper or showing irritation because she did not want to spoil the day by insulting Vashiri bridal traditions or rejecting them. After all, there was no doubt whatsoever that her female companions, virtually none of whom spoke English, were overjoyed that their king was getting married again. That she was a foreigner did not appear to be a stumbling block in any way.

'Ella!' A female voice carolled from the doorway and Ella glanced up to see Cristo Ravelli's vibrant wife, Belle, with her mane of wild Titian hair, surging towards her and she grinned because it was quite impossible to do anything else. Although she had met Zarif's brothers and their wives on only one previous occasion she had not forgotten Belle with her warm Irish friendliness, or the quieter but no less sociable Betsy, because at the time she had met them—*before* Zarif's proposal—she had been fantasising that some day she would become a part of their close-knit family circle as well.

'I thought we were never going to get through all the obstacles being put up to us joining you up here!' Belle exclaimed, settling a heap of gift-wrapped packages and an enormous tote bag down carelessly on the floor. 'This is my first visit to this palace. I had no idea it was still running at about five hundred years behind the times.'

'Belle...' Tiny blonde Betsy emerged from behind Belle and bent down to kiss Ella's cheek in greeting. 'How are you bearing up?'

'Oh, don't waste time asking her that!' Belle exclaimed. 'No, we're more interested in hearing why you said no three years ago and are now suddenly saying yes to our Desert King.'

Ella froze at that blunt question, which was, nonetheless, perfectly understandable in the circumstances. 'That would be a...er...challenging story to tell. Hanya,' she murmured, seeing the pretty brunette hovering with a suspiciously stiff look on her face as if she resented the intrusion of the two Western women. 'Could we have some drinks and snacks for Zarif's family, please?'

'I thought the whole palace was dry,' Belle commented out of the corner of her mouth. 'Not that Zarif doesn't take the occasional alcoholic drink, but the old boy who's ill never touches a drop of the evil stuff.'

'If you put your foot in your mouth one more

time I'm not going to fish you out of it!' Betsy warned her companion on the back of a groan. 'Ella, we're here to provide support.'

'We're here to celebrate!' Belle contradicted. '*Why* would Ella need support? She's marrying a gorgeous billionaire who's also a reigning king and obviously he's madly in love with her because I'm shocked he's forgiven her for rejecting him the first time around!'

'No, he's not madly in love with me and I'm not sure he's forgiven me either,' Ella heard herself admit flatly as glasses of pomegranate juice and a tray of little appetisers were handed round. Belle wrinkled her nose at the lack of stronger spirit in her beverage.

'Cheers,' Belle pronounced nonetheless, knocking her glass noisily against Ella's. 'Cristo wasn't in love with me when we got married either, so don't worry about it. That came afterwards and surprised us both. I married him to get a name and security for our half-siblings and he married me to stop me going to court to fight for their rights. But I know Zarif...he *has* to be in love.'

'Why?' Ella asked baldly before tucking into a

tiny delicious appetiser consisting of a mini pastry case and a mousse filling.

'Because all this is happening so fast. It's just *not* Zarif. He's usually so cool and right now he's acting all hot-headed and spontaneous.'

'That is true.' Betsy too was looking thoughtful.

Hanya intervened to tell Ella that it was time for her to get dressed. An elaborate kaftan was displayed to her along with a silk chemise composed of several voluminous layers while Hanya added that underwear was not traditionally worn.

Belle frowned when she saw Ella's expression of dismay and stooped down to her collection of parcels to retrieve one and present it to Ella with a flourish. 'One of my gifts is some pretty lingerie. The bride has to wear something new, Hanya. It's one of *our* traditions and going naked beneath a petticoat isn't.'

Ella vanished into the giant Victorian bathroom with the gift box and wrenched it open to pull out a handful of pristine white lace, the sort of fancy underpinnings she had never worn in her life but the prospect of wearing them was infinitely preferable to going bare, with large breasts that felt uncomfortable without support. She put them on in a rush, fearful that at any moment the door, which did not have a lock, would open because her tribe of watchful Vashiri companions did not seem to have much idea that a woman might want privacy from an audience. Pulling the robe back on, she returned to the huge bedroom.

Within the space of a minute the heavy kaftan was being swiftly dropped over her head, the hooks fastened and the satin ribbon ties tightened to fit. The elaborate hand-done embroidery on the sky-blue fabric was truly magnificent.

'That doesn't look half bad,' Belle began in evident surprise.

'It's beautiful…especially with your colouring,' Betsy cut in with an admiring smile.

Ella sat down in a chair while her hair was brushed. 'I'll do my own make-up,' she told Hanya firmly when extravagant compacts of very brightly coloured eye shadows were unfurled threateningly in front of her. 'Zarif doesn't like a lot of make-up.'

And then she thought, Why am I thinking like

that, as though I *want* to make myself more attractive for him? Where did that weird thought come from? Had it been born in the moment when with only a little elementary foreplay Zarif had sent her careening into an explosive climax, giving her more pleasure than she had ever dreamt was possible? Her cheeks burned with mortification.

Belle thrust a glass into her hand. *'Enjoy,'* she urged. 'Don't let Hanya bully you.'

'I'm not timid. I'm just very reluctant to do or say anything that might offend anyone,' Ella confided wryly as she sipped and munched on another appetiser. 'And she *has* to know the right way to do everything here because she was Azel's cousin.'

'And unless I'm very much mistaken, she was exceedingly hopeful that Zarif would marry her, *not* you. I sense a generous helping of the old green monster envy every time she looks at you,' Belle spelt out in her ear.

Ella's eyes rounded as she did her make-up. 'But I won't ever measure up to Azel,' she muttered in rueful acceptance.

'First wife still casting a big shadow in the present, is she?' Betsy murmured. 'You shouldn't let that bother you. I mean, it's not as if Zarif *chose* to marry her. He was *told* he would be marrying her when he was only a kid. It was set in stone, an arranged marriage—no romance there or any room to act on his own feelings in such a rigid set-up. You were the very *first* woman he went on a date with and *he chose you…*'

He chose you. It was a different take on Zarif's history, which Ella had not previously considered, and she was grateful for it. Her shadowed eyes suddenly brightened and she laughed, unable to kill the smile creeping across her formerly tense mouth. 'Are you serious?'

'Very. Zarif was married at eighteen and he was a virgin when he got married. Nik and Cristo tried to persuade him to wait longer before tying the knot but Zarif followed his grandfather's dictates and he always puts his duty to his country first. Let's face it, all Zarif's advisors were mad keen to marry him off to a suitable woman asap, particularly once he began connecting with his half-brothers from the West. When he met you three years ago, we were all really happy for him.'

Ella stiffened and wielded her mascara brush with great care. 'It didn't work out.'

'None of us understand why. It was *so* obvious you were mad about him when we first met,' Belle told her bluntly. 'You couldn't take your eyes off him. It was kind of sweet.'

In chagrined silence, Ella swallowed more of her drink and Belle topped it up with a tall bottle that had come out of nowhere. 'What's that?' she asked.

'Vodka. I had it in my bag. I'm not swearing off drink at a wedding,' Belle declared defiantly.

'I shouldn't have too much… I haven't much of a head for alcohol,' Ella admitted.

Her make-up done, Ella stayed still while an elaborate coin-hung headdress was anchored to her brow. Then it was time to gaze in a full-length mirror at the vision of exotic splendour she had become in her opulent royal regalia.

'Now we go and view some ceremonial sword dance,' Belle announced cheerfully, having had a discussion with a very disapproving Hanya while urging Ella towards the door and slotting her glass back in her hand. 'Drink up. I haven't yet given up hope that I can transform you into a *happy* bride.'

Guilt assailed Ella as she realised she had not been putting on a good enough show to make the expected impression. *A happy bride?* No indeed. But, these women were members of Zarif's family and she should've been trying harder. 'I'm sorry, I'm—'

'No worries,' tiny Betsy whispered, squeezing her arm comfortingly. 'Weddings are ninety-nine per cent stress even without cultural differences involved.'

'But thanks to our objections you're not going to be sentenced to a female-only reception,' Belle broke in with satisfaction. 'For the first time ever, a palace wedding will be a mixed gathering. We talked Zarif into it last night and he admitted that many of his subjects have long since abandoned all this dated separating-the-sexes-stuff. If you ask me, you can blame his uncle for all the old-fashioned stuff around here. Nobody wants to tread on *his* toes.'

'Hush…' Ella urged, skimming concerned eyes at the forthright redhead while she rubbed her aching brow with a fleeting brush of her fingers because she was starting to get what she assumed to be a tension headache. 'Zarif is very attached to his uncle Halim and he's seriously ill.'

'If you can't say something nice, say nothing,' Betsy advised. 'Ella's not used to you yet.'

'But I do like and respect honesty,' Ella admitted, following Hanya out onto a large stone balcony. A large group of men wielding swords and clad in white traditional robes were lined up in the courtyard below. Towards the rear she could see Nik and Cristo, Zarif's brothers, standing in the shade to watch. Zarif was easiest of all to pick out of the crowd. He wore magnificent gold-coloured robes that glimmered in the brilliant sunshine. A belt with an ornate golden dagger thrust through it accentuated his narrow waist. His white *kaffiyeh* was bound with a double gold cord and, framed by that pale backdrop, his hard bronzed features were shockingly handsome. It was all very solemn and serious. A drum beat sounded and the lines of men shifted their feet at a rhythmic pace, roared something incomprehensible and lunged forward with their swords.

'Could we have just five minutes alone with our sister?' Belle asked Hanya pleadingly.

With a look of deep resentment, the young Vashiri woman backed into the corridor and Belle shut the door on her while heaving a sigh of relief. 'Of course you can't talk with her listening in!'

Ella drank from her glass. She felt incredibly thirsty, her mouth very dry as she watched Zarif leap across the central fire pit with astonishing athleticism and grace, his lean, muscular body soaring high above the flames. At that moment he simply took her breath away.

'He's so fit and he's probably been doing that stuff since he was about five years old,' Betsy commented admiringly. 'Nik said he had a very traditional upbringing with his grandparents and his uncle.'

Belle was scanning Ella's expressive face as she watched her handsome bridegroom bring down his sword with a metallic clash to meet the other men's weapons in the inner circle. 'Why on earth did you reject him three years ago?'

'None of our business,' Betsy slotted in uneasily.

'He told me he would always love Azel and that she was irreplaceable,' Ella heard herself admit before she could think better of it.

'You're kidding me,' Belle breathed, her face stunned. 'I can't believe he was that stu—'

'At least he was honest,' Ella countered defensively. 'It wasn't what I wanted to hear but I was better off knowing.'

'Men!' Belle exclaimed in a tone of lingering disbelief as Ella opened the door to invite Hanya back in to join them. Ella was annoyed with herself for speaking so freely and reckoned that Hanya's deflating presence would, at least, make her guard her tongue.

When the dance was finished, Ella's mind was stuffed with exotic imagery of Zarif as she had never seen him before. Hanya led them downstairs into an ornately tiled room where Zarif was waiting with his brothers, the imam and an older man in a wheelchair with a nurse hovering over him. Halim al-Rastani's poor state of health was obvious in his sunken dark eyes and pallor but he smiled warmly at Ella and he lifted a frail hand to urge her to come closer.

Lean, strong face grave, Zarif moved forward to join her and perform a formal introduction.

'You are indeed very beautiful,' Zarif's uncle told her kindly. 'It is a joy for me to meet you at last. May you and my nephew be blessed with many children and a long life.'

Momentarily colliding with Zarif's warning golden gaze and feeling rather as though she had run into a brick wall, Ella swallowed hard and lowered her lashes. Quite ridiculously she felt guilty about the reality that she had no intention of having any children with Zarif and indeed was currently taking medication that should prevent pregnancy. Her head was also beginning to swim a little. It had to be the heat getting to her, she thought ruefully, perspiration dampening her upper lip. The palace had ceiling fans everywhere but no proper air conditioning and she was sweltering in the heavy kaftan layered with petticoats.

The imam stepped forward and began to speak while Betsy's husband, Nik, stationed himself to Ella's left side and quietly and smoothly translated every word of the Arabic ceremony for her benefit. A guiding hand resting in the shallow indentation of her spine, Zarif led her over to the table where a document awaited their signatures.

'The marriage contract,' Zarif explained as the witnesses followed suit. He lifted a large and ornate wooden box from the table and extended it to Ella.

'What's this?' she whispered, leaning slightly sideways at the sheer weight of the box.

'It's the *mahr*...your dowry,' Nik translated with some amusement.

Hamid darted forward to remove the box from Ella's hold and bestow it on Hanya, who was waiting outside the door.

'I have a *dowry*?' Ella muttered to Zarif, her disbelief at the explanation unconcealed.

One hand cupping her elbow, Zarif drew her into an alcove off the corridor. His lean, extravagantly handsome face was forbidding in its uninformative stillness. 'It is traditional that I give my bride the royal jewel collection.'

'But you've already given my family so much,' Ella muttered in growing discomfiture.

'That is our private business. I sincerely doubt that you want that fact spread round my entire family,' Zarif spelt out very drily. 'I'm sure I need not add that you must surrender the jewels when we part.'

Her face flamed hotter than a fire in embarrassment and she tore her discomfited gaze from his lean, darkly handsome features, embarrassment and resentment creating a heady tempest of reaction inside her. 'I'm not stupid,' she declared, wrenching her arm free of his and leaving the alcove to join Hanya where she waited with the box several feet away.

'Your Majesty.' Hanya curtsied to her for the first time and ushered Ella into another room. 'You will want to put on some jewellery before you meet your guests.'

In actuality there was nothing Ella wanted to do less than don any piece of jewellery that was only on loan to her until Zarif took a *real* wife and which had previously been worn by Azel. How dared he assume that she would have the cheek to try and retain valuables that did not belong to her after their fake marriage ended? Pride brought her chin up but she thought better of protest and compressed her lips, leaving Hanya to the task of selecting items from the overflowing casket of glittering gold-encased gems.

Decked out, in her own opinion, like a Christmas tree, Ella followed Hanya slowly into the vast reception room where all the guests were gathered. Hanya left her hovering just inside the doorway and approached Zarif. Ella watched the dainty brunette speak to her tall, powerfully built husband and wondered what Azel's cousin was saying to stamp such a look of brooding dissatisfaction on Zarif's lean, strong face. Ella joined Belle, who admired the collar of flawless sapphires encircling Ella's elegant neck and the superb matching pendant earrings reaching almost to her shoulder.

'Wow,' Belle breathed in reverent admiration. 'I've seen loads of jewels but in all my life I've never seen anything to equal the size and clarity of those.'

Zarif studied his bride, whose gait was almost imperceptibly unsteady. His expressive mouth tightened. While the famous sapphires certainly enhanced the breathtaking gentian blue of her eyes, the feverish colour highlighting her cheekbones and the pallor of her porcelain skin beyond it were equally obvious to him. Most probably the large amount of alcohol she had consumed was having an effect, he thought derisively, furious that she could have been so foolish as to indulge in such a dangerous practice when their behaviour was the focus of every person present.

One hand on her elbow as guidance, he escorted her round the room to introduce her to local dignitaries and then he took her through to the banqueting room where the wedding meal was being staged.

Ella was feeling very hot, literally as though she were burning up below the kaftan. There was a sensation of tightness across her chest and her breath was wheezing and catching a little in her throat. The jewellery was as heavy as the dress and she felt dizzy and slightly nauseous. 'I think I need to sit down,' she told Zarif before he could make her talk to any more strangers.

A pair of throne-like chairs sat below a canopy and he settled her down in one with great care. 'Food will be brought to us,' he informed her, taking a seat by her side.

Ella had never felt less hungry in her life. Indeed the prospect of food turned her stomach. There was a metallic taste in her mouth and her throat felt funny. Strong black coffee was served to her by a kneeling servant.

'Coffee will sober you up,' Zarif pronounced with lethal derision.

'I'm not drunk…I only had *one* drink,' Ella whispered back at him, staring at him in consternation and surprise. 'And I don't feel like coffee.'

'Drink it,' Zarif instructed in a raw aside.

Ella felt more like throwing it at him but, conscious that they were the cynosure of attention, she sipped doggedly at the bitter brew, hoping it would ease her tight throat. Unfortunately the coffee seemed to exacerbate her nausea and before very long she flew upright without a word to Zarif and headed off in urgent search of the nearest cloakroom.

'Where are you going?' he demanded, catching her hand in his to still her in her tracks.

'Cloakroom…*sick*!' she gasped in desperation.

He urged her out through a side door with a scantily leashed curse. 'In there…' he told her grimly.

In merciful privacy, Ella lost the meagre contents of her stomach and then hung on the edge of the vanity unit to stay upright while she tried to freshen her mouth. Cramping pains continued to course across her abdomen. She was feeling really ill and she staggered slightly as she reeled dizzily back to Zarif's side. 'I'm not well,' she muttered shakily, feeling hot and cold and dreadful, black spots appearing in her vision.

'You will have to control it,' Zarif informed her unsympathetically.

Her head swimming, her legs hollow and weak, Ella gave him an incredulous glance from heavily lidded eyes and then she dropped like a stone to the tiled floor at his feet.

CHAPTER SIX

ZARIF STUDIED HIS BRIDE, his stern gaze welded to the still slight figure in the big bed. Recent events had made certain facts painfully clear: Ella was his wife and his to protect. *His* responsibility alone. And he had almost lost her, indeed come within minutes of doing so and he was still in shock from the experience.

Had he known what he was doing when he married her? Had he really believed he could shrug off all sense of obligation and sidestep the commitment? So what if, once, she had played games with him and hurt his pride? She had only been a girl, a fickle, lively girl playing with fire without knowing she could get burned. And yet he *had* intended to burn her, had intended to punish her.

His wide sensual mouth compressed on the acknowledgement that everything had changed in the space of a moment, the same moment in which Ella had collapsed at his feet. He had made a grievous error of judgement and it could have cost Ella her life. He did not want to picture a world in which Ella no longer walked. His bitterness was not so deep, his pride not so high. He still wanted her more than he had ever wanted a woman and he could not let her go, he *would* not let her go until he was free of his craving for her. Only then could he move on and remarry, awarding his next wife the full unquestioning commitment that was her due.

Ella's eyelashes fluttered and then lifted on a dimly lit room.

An ornate canopy hung over the bed. The edges of the fabric were fringed and tasselled and swinging a little in the breeze. She identified the source of the breeze as the whirring fan in the background and put a hand up to discover what was covering her nose.

'Don't touch the oxygen mask!' Zarif warned her, suddenly appearing by the side of the bed and giving her a fright.

Ella blinked up at him as though he were a

mirage. Muddled and confusing images of the sword dance, the wedding and the guests were racing through her mind faster than the speed of light until she recalled the last ignominious moment in the cloakroom, after which everything became a complete blank.

'What happened?' she whispered limply, focusing on his lean, darkly handsome face, paying special notice to the black spiky lashes that heightened the effect of his stunning dark golden eyes. Evidently, his mood hadn't improved because he still looked bleak and forbidding as hell.

Disconcertingly, Zarif sank down with confusing informality on the side of the bed and closed an imprisoning hand over hers as it crept inexorably towards the irritating oxygen mask again. 'You almost died.'

'That's not possible,' Ella told him, shifting her arm and only then noticing the IV attached.

'We believe you are allergic to shellfish.'

'I'm not allergic to shellfish. I'm not allergic to anything,' Ella proclaimed.

'You may not have been until today but you *are* allergic now. The shellfish pastries you ate before the wedding are the most likely explanation and when you are better you will undergo tests so that we can discover what it is safe for you to eat. You went into anaphylactic shock. I thought you were drunk...and all the time you were *ill*,' Zarif breathed in a hoarse undertone of remorse, dark eyes blazing gold over her flushed face, his lean hand tightening over hers. 'If Halim's doctor had not been present and able to administer an immediate shot of adrenalin, you could have gone into cardiac arrest.'

Ella breathed in slow and deep. 'But I didn't. I'm fine,' she told him quietly. 'What a thing to happen in public—you must've been very embarrassed.'

'Embarrassment was the least of my concerns,' Zarif admitted. 'I wronged you. I made an unjust assumption and you suffered for it. Hanya told me you'd drunk a lot of alcohol.'

Ella stiffened. 'That *is* a lie. Belle gave me one drink. It may have been a large drink but there was only one and I didn't finish it.'

'It is immaterial. I should naturally have given you the benefit of the doubt. It is my duty to look after you and I failed and it could have cost you your life,' he breathed harshly.

'How on earth could you have known that I was going to suffer a severe allergic reaction to something I ate?' Ella asked ruefully. 'It's not your fault. It's not anyone's fault. It was just bad luck.'

'Nonetheless, we will be very, very careful about what you eat in the future,' Zarif decreed. 'Dr Mansour warned me that another attack could be fatal. He asked me to call him as soon as you wake up.'

In a daze, Ella watched Zarif unfurl his cell phone and within minutes the middle-aged doctor put in an appearance. He confirmed that it was possible to suddenly become allergic to a substance that one might have eaten for years without ill effects but while urging her to exercise caution he was considerably less dramatic about her prospects than Zarif had been. Zarif, Ella registered, was in still in shock at her collapse and blaming himself for it. The oxygen mask removed because she was breathing easily and the IV removed because she faithfully promised to drink lots of water, she levered herself up against the pillows once they were alone again.

'I'm sorry about all this,' she murmured awkwardly. 'I suppose it's no use telling you that I'm usually as healthy as a horse.'

'I owe you an apology,' Zarif murmured tautly. 'I misjudged you. I should have realised that you were genuinely ill.'

'How could you have?' Ella parried uneasily. 'I didn't realise what was wrong with me either.'

'You need to rest now,' Zarif told her simply. 'Could you eat something first? You've had very little today.'

Ella identified the hollow sensation inside her as hunger and smiled ruefully. 'Yes, I am hungry.'

Servants brought food while Ella watched Zarif from below her lashes. He had removed his headdress and his luxuriant black hair was tousled as though he had run his fingers through it several times. He needed a shave as well, black stubble cloaking his stubborn jawline and somehow highlighting the effect of his beautifully modelled mouth. In truth, still clad in the gold robes that glimmered richly even in the lamp light, he looked utterly amazing and beautiful and she simply couldn't take her eyes off him.

'You should've stayed with your guests,' Ella remarked uncomfortably, struggling to rein in her overpowering reaction to his lean, lithe, dark good looks.

'I'm your husband. You should always be my first priority,' Zarif fielded in surprise. 'What sort of husband would behave otherwise?'

Ella was silenced while she mulled over that response. He certainly seemed to feel a lot more married than he had the day before. Was that a good thing or a bad thing? She wasn't sure. She picked pieces from the various dishes spread on trays around her on the bed and ate with an appetite that surprised her. When Belle and Betsy arrived to visit her, she greeted them with an apologetic wince.

'I'm a real party pooper, aren't I?' she sighed.

'I should never have given you that vodka,' Belle commented guiltily. 'It's my fault that Zarif initially assumed that you were tipsy.'

'I'd blame Hanya,' Betsy said, disconcerting

Ella with that frank opinion. 'I think she convinced Zarif that you had drunk enough to be dancing on tables. She quite deliberately misled him to make you look bad.'

'But those stupid prawn appetisers would have wrecked your wedding night anyway,' Belle pointed out sympathetically. 'And at least Zarif knows the truth now.'

It was only then that it actually occurred to Ella that it *was* her wedding night and she flushed, amazed that she had so easily forgotten what had earlier dominated her every thought. She exchanged fond goodbyes with her new sisters-in-law and promised to visit them when she was next in London—whenever that might be. As they departed she slid out of the high bed, keen to go for a shower and freshen up. That was when Zarif chose to reappear.

'I'm going for a shower,' she told him tightly, murderously conscious of the horribly old-fashioned and shapeless white nightdress that she had been put in after her collapse and hoping very much that Zarif had not been involved in undressing her.

Zarif scanned her tense figure and anxious face. Sheathed in a white cotton gown that could only have belonged to someone either very old or very modest, she looked like an angel with her wealth of blonde hair tumbling round her shoulders and her blue eyes big and bright above her pink cheeks. Doubtless she was worried that he might be selfish enough to try and claim his marital rights regardless of her weakened condition and he straightened his broad shoulders.

'I'll sleep elsewhere tonight,' he told her flatly.

Ella added two and two and made four. 'This is *your* room?'

Zarif nodded, brilliant dark golden eyes veiled as if he was reluctant to remind her that she was his wife and that this was their wedding night.

'I wouldn't dream of putting you out of your room,' Ella declared, tense with discomfiture and determined not to prove any more of a nuisance than she had already been. 'Stay—we're grown-ups, surely we can share the bed?'

Without another word, she vanished into the bathroom, which she was relieved to discover was infinitely more modern than the one she had used at the start of the day. Indeed the jets from the power shower stung her out of her lethargy and soon had her reaching for a towel. She had no choice other than to don the same old-fashioned nightie when she was dry. The bedroom was empty when she emerged and she wasted no time in climbing into the bed.

About ten minutes later, Zarif returned to the bedroom, naked but for the towel knotted round his narrow hips. Water droplets still clung to the dark curls of hair scattered across his virile pecs and his hair was still damp, spiked up by a rough towelling. Her attention roamed to the muscled planes of his strong brown back and lean hips before straying without her volition to his heavily muscled torso and the hard, corrugated slab of his flat stomach.

Her mouth ran dry as he extracted something from a drawer and let the towel drop carelessly to the floor, exposing taut brown buttocks. Muscles rippling, he yanked on a pair of black boxers and she suddenly closed her eyes tight, embarrassed that she had been spying on him, ashamed that she could be twenty-four years old and still that naively curious about the male body.

Wouldn't everything have been easier had she been more experienced? Sleeping with Zarif would then have been no big deal, she told herself. Only to change her mind as she lifted her lashes half a sneaky inch and watched him stroll towards the bed with the predatory grace of a prowling panther, almost stopping her heart dead with excitement in the process. She swallowed hard as he doused the lights and the bed gave beneath his weight.

'You know if you want to, you can…I'm feeling fine now,' she told him with startling abruptness, utterly fed up with the ridiculous level of nervous tension he inspired in her and ready to do virtually anything to put it to flight.

Perplexed by that unexpected offer, Zarif flipped over on his side to peer at her, his dark eyes gleaming in the moonlight. 'I can wait until you're back to full strength. After the day we've had, you must be tired. I know I am.'

Heat surged up from Ella's throat to her hairline and mortification almost choked her. She gritted her teeth. So, he was too tired to be tempted by her. Well, she had offered and he had turned her down. Let it not be said that she could not take rejection on the chin. Punching the pillow beneath her head, she turned her back on him and curled up, eyes wide and stinging like mad.

When Ella wakened she was alone in the big bed. Rising, she went through the closets and drawers until she found her own clothing. Leaving out lingerie and a sundress, she went into the bathroom to freshen up. When she emerged wrapped in a towel, a maid was changing the bed and as soon as she saw Ella the young woman curtsied and swept open a communicating door to indicate the table laden with dishes in the room next door.

'Good morning, *habibti*,' Zarif drawled, springing upright from the table.

Ella hovered. 'Good morning. I'd better get dressed.'

'There is no need. We won't be disturbed and I would assume that you don't want *cold* hot chocolate.'

Taste buds watering, Ella took a step forward. 'You have hot chocolate?'

A wolfish grin slashed Zarif's darkly handsome features and his tawny eyes gleamed. 'I have hot chocolate and croissants for you…'

Ella gave him a huge natural smile and closed the door behind her, tucking in the towel knotted above her breasts and sinking down into a chair. 'When did you get up?'

'I go into the office about six and answer my emails while it's quiet. I like to enjoy a leisurely breakfast.' He poured the hot chocolate and the rich aroma of it made her sniff in appreciation as she reached for a croissant.

Ella was disconcerted that he had remembered two of her favourite things. The past beckoned and she struggled to fend off memories of their bittersweet time together three years earlier. Back then she had been utterly convinced that he was a romantic and she had been so much in love that even the feel of his hand enclosing hers had lit her up inside like a firework display. She blinked, pushing away the unproductive memories and all recollection of the dreaming, trusting girl she had been. Then as now, she told herself, it had *all* been about sex and she had better not forget that for a moment.

Zarif withdrew the ring box from his pocket and set it in front of her. 'I intended to give this to you yesterday but there was no opportunity.'

Ella opened the box to stare down at the magnificent sapphire and diamond ring. 'What's it for?'

'I heard the child at our English wedding ask why you had no engagement ring. I bought it for you three years ago,' Zarif admitted ruefully.

'And you don't mind me wearing it?' Ella had flushed. He had very much disconcerted her.

'I want you to wear it, *habibti*. It was always meant to be yours.'

Ella slid on the ring. It was a perfect fit. He had kept it for three years, maybe even forgotten he still had it until a child's chatter had reminded him. He was being practical, that was all. He would hardly want to give the ring he had chosen for her to another woman in the future. 'It's gorgeous. Thank you,' she said quietly.

Zarif liked looking at the two wedding rings

and the engagement ring on her slender finger. She was his at last, a surprisingly soothing
thought. He watched her eat the croissant, crumbs
scattering while a look of delight slowly wakened on her lovely face. Within seconds he was
hot and hard and when she sipped the chocolate,
just a hint of the sweet drink coating her full, soft
lower lip as she emitted a soft moan of pleasure,
he was ready to rip her out of the chair and carry
her to bed. Suddenly all he could think about
was seeing that expression on her face while he
pleasured her.

'I want you…' he husked.

Ella froze like a cornered kitten, blue eyes flying wide as she stared back at him, a tiny pulse
beating like crazy just above her collarbone.

'I meant to wait…I intended to wait,' Zarif confided thickly as he sprang gracefully upright.
'But when I look at you, I *can't*.'

Her mouth ran dry while the blood in her veins
ran hotter than lava. He towered over her, all
male, decidedly exotic and stunningly sexy in
his pristine robes. Her gaze locked tight to him,
her heartbeat quickening, her breath feathering in

her throat while her lungs laboured to fill again. That stillness, that primal sexual awareness that engulfed her was exactly what had made mincemeat of her principles when she had first met him. It shocked her that that could happen to her again, cutting through her new maturity, her bitterness and distrust to leave only the mindless yearning she had once suppressed.

As Ella began to rise from her seat Zarif bent his head and claimed a long, intense kiss. His tongue skated across hers and a piercing dart of such primitive longing slithered through her that it was a challenge to stay upright. A strong arm slid to her spine to support her slender frame and he lifted her off her feet with breathtaking ease to carry her back into the bedroom.

CHAPTER SEVEN

ELLA SURFACED TO find herself lying on the bed. After that burning kiss she felt a little as if she had been hit with a brick because her brain no longer felt as if it were functioning. Zarif was poised several feet away, stripping off his robes and letting them fall on the rug, his proud dark head already bare. Ella breathed in slow and deep.

It was time, she told her quailing nerves firmly. They were married. This was the deal she had made. Neither love nor liking came into the arrangement. Sex was on the menu, nothing else, and she had to learn to be practical about the fact.

Naked but for his boxers, Zarif was an intimidating sight, a literal power-house of whipcord muscle overlaid with smooth bronzed skin. Her intent gaze skated down over the steely muscles of his formidable chest, down over the little furrow of soft dark hair disappearing below the waistband of his boxers, and screeched to a sudden halt. The bulge of his straining masculinity was larger than she had expected and she tensed, telling herself not to be silly, not to get all worked up about something that other women took in their stride. She wasn't a child. She might not have had sex before but she was an educated adult and none of her friends had been swept off to paradise by their first-time experience. Once it was done, though, it was done, she bargained with herself, desperate to establish a calmer outlook. Afterwards she would know what all the fuss was about and she would be able to treat such intimacy as a mundane event.

'I've wanted you for so long,' Zarif admitted, running long supple fingers through the swirling spill of her honey-coloured hair across the pillows. 'You're so beautiful...'

Ella very nearly laughed. She could see herself as pretty on a good day but only when she was all done up and her hair absolutely perfect. Certainly she did not compare well to the true beauties she had seen him pictured with in newspapers three years earlier. Zarif was the truly beautiful one, an outstandingly gorgeous male, who had stolen her heart the first time she saw him and broken it the day he proposed, sending her plunging from the heights of happiness straight down into the darkness of despair. In the aftermath she had picked herself up and gone on but the trust he had broken remained broken and she was a much more anxious, suspicious person than she had once been.

His thick silky hair nudged her cheek and then his mouth, velvet and warm, claimed hers again, closing out the rest of the world as though it had never been. There was nothing then but the racing beat of her heart and the tightening at her secret core. Without warning the towel she wore was gone and he cupped her full breasts, his thumbs strumming her engorged nipples to send currents of fire shooting down into her pelvis. Her hips shifted, rose without her volition and at the heart of her she felt tight as a drum and desperate for more.

Zarif drew back, lean, strong features taut. 'If you truly don't want this, I will stop. I don't want anything from you that you don't want to give, *habibti.*'

Taken aback, Ella stared up at him, still partially lost in the stirring responses shimmying through her lethargic body.

Luxuriant black lashes dipped low over his tawny eyes. 'You didn't want this,' he extended. 'You agreed because you had no other choice but I find that I no longer want a sacrifice in my bed.'

Disconcerted, Ella stiffened. 'I'm *not* a sacrifice.'

His mouth dipped to her delicate collarbone and the tip of his tongue flicked the pulse beating there below her pale fine skin and she tingled in reaction from her head to her toes. 'I will have you willing or not at all. To say no is your right and I promise that there will be no reprisals,' he asserted thickly.

In shock at that startling offer coming when she least expected it, Ella opened her eyes to their fullest extent and stared up at him, almost mesmerised by the stunning amber gold of his steady gaze. 'But I agreed and you—'

'You agreed under the duress of your concern

for your vulnerable parents,' Zarif reminded her. 'And I am man enough to only want what is offered freely.'

His hands rested on her ribcage and she wanted so badly for him to lift his hands and touch her breasts again. The strength of that craving took her aback for nothing in her experience had ever equalled it. She shut her eyes, shutting him out but the craving, the sheer hunger mushroomed up inside her without abating. And why was she surprised? She wanted him; she had *always* wanted him.

Her lashes lifted, her decision easily made. 'It's free...I mean, it's only sex...let's not make a production out of it,' she framed awkwardly.

Zarif frowned in disagreement, automatically writing off her quip about sex as a clumsy careless joke. 'I very much want it to be a production with you, *habibti.*'

Ella lay back, pliant and melting with helpless anticipation. She had come to an understanding with herself and the past and present were melding into a seamless whole. She wanted Zarif to become her first lover because she had never wanted another man the way she wanted him and sharing her body with him made perfect sense to her. He nipped at her lower lip and then blew softly over a rosy straining nipple before suckling erotically at the tender peak. Ribbons of hot desire pulled taut between her breasts and her thighs.

Zarif slid down the bed, tugging away the towel still partially wrapped round her and skimming off the boxers he still wore with impatient hands. Lying there naked, Ella reddened, fighting off the urge to yank the sheet over her exposed body. He parted her thighs and before she could react moved down the bed towards her on his knees with the predatory grace of a stalking cat. Ella lay still, eyes rounding when she glimpsed the long thick length of his erection hung low between his muscular hair-roughened thighs. A spasm of something she didn't recognise pulled taut in her pelvis.

Zarif dropped a kiss on her gently rounded stomach and tension leapt high inside her as he stroked the soft skin of her inner thighs, moving ever closer to the heart of her desire. 'I want to taste you,' he told her hungrily. 'I want to drive you crazy with need and then I want to make love to you until you are senseless…'

'A lot of wants,' she pronounced shakily, shy of that new side of him and the raw sexual self-assurance she had never seen him display before.

'And all the time in the world in which to enjoy them,' Zarif murmured, pushing her slender thighs back at almost the same time as he lowered his head and swiped his tongue across her clitoris.

The sensation was so powerful that she almost shot off the bed in shock. 'No…no, you *can't* do that!' she told him when she had found her breath again.

'You'll discover that I am naturally domineering in the bedroom,' Zarif confessed without apology, his strong hands clamping to her hips to hold her in place for his attentions.

'I've…I've just never quite…' Ella mumbled unevenly.

'But your body loves it and so do I,' Zarif countered hungrily, marvelling that an experienced woman could have such an inhibition while he ran long fingers soothingly down the outside of her slender thighs to relax her tense muscles. 'Close your eyes…I promise only pleasure, *habibti.*'

Afraid of making a fool of herself and entering into an undignified tussle, Ella shut her eyes tight, mentally willing herself to play it cool. She really didn't want Zarif to know that she hadn't done any of these things before. If he realised she was still a virgin he might then appreciate what a catastrophic effect he had had on her life three years earlier and her pride was too great to reveal the massive hurt he had unwittingly inflicted.

He teased the entrance to her body with gentle fingertips and she jerked, insanely conscious of where she needed to be touched and cringingly aware of how wet she was. He eased a finger into her and then lowered his head to tease her with his sensual mouth. Almost unbearable sensation engulfed Ella in a never-ending cascade. She no longer controlled herself; *he* controlled her. Her body hummed and jerked with constrained power like a race car at the starting line, raring to go. Excitement roared through every cell in her body, drowning all thought, closing out everything but what he was making her feel. The ripples of growing sensation soared to a peak and her back arched and she cried out while ripples of pleasure spread outward, making the pleasure last and draining every ounce of energy from her body.

'I have no condoms here,' Zarif groaned in frustration and he levered himself off the bed.

Ella blinked as she struggled to emerge from that frighteningly intense climax and suddenly reached out to close a hand over his before he could move out of reach. 'I'm on the pill…it's safe,' she muttered, assuming it would be safe, then certain it was because she had, after all, been taking the mini pill for years to regulate her periods and surely all those years had to count for something.

For a split second, Zarif hesitated and then he came back to her with alacrity. 'It's a very long time since I had sex without a condom,' he confided, pulling her close to his warm, musky male length, his erection pressing against her lower stomach. In that instant her hunger for him rose to such a height that she felt weak and dizzy with it.

'You can be assured that I am clean and healthy,' he murmured, studying her with scorching dark golden eyes fringed by quite ridiculously long black lashes. 'And you?'

'I've never had sex without a condom,' Ella replied, trying not to laugh because, of course, she had never had sex at all but she was convinced he would not be able to tell the difference between her untried body and a more practised woman's.

He captured her lips in a soul-shattering kiss and deep down inside her the tingling and the prickle of awakening heat and the awful aching emptiness began to fire her up afresh. He was so hot, she reflected helplessly, so hot that he made her crave him like a sunburn victim craved ice. She quivered below the hard, warm weight of his lean, powerful body, entranced by the intimacy but nervous of what the next step entailed, regardless of how much her body seemed to yearn for it.

He tilted her up to facilitate his entry and nudged at her entrance before pushing in, filling her completely and stilling to give her time to adjust.

'You're very small,' Zarif husked, his black hair brushing her cheek. 'I don't want to hurt you.'

Ella was all bound up in the alien sensation of his intrusion in that wildly sensitive place and in the same moment he pulled back and then drove forward, thrusting into her with primal force. A strangled shriek of shocked pain escaped her and he froze over her.

'What the hell?' he breathed rawly, frowning down at her in consternation.

Ella gulped and regrouped. 'It's been a while for me,' she told him weakly.

Ebony brows pleated, Zarif began to withdraw and her hands whipped up instinctively to close over his muscular forearms even as her hips lifted to contain him. 'No, don't stop,' she protested, incredulous at the idea that he could go so far and then stop without letting her experience what she had ached to share only with him for so long.

That would be another rejection and just then she couldn't face that prospect; no, not to be left with the suspicion that she was so much less than other women and so useless that she could not retain his interest even until the act was finished. She could not bear that her only sexual experience should end in failure and shame.

The muscles in his arms strained and Zarif groaned, fighting for control until the shift of her hips embraced him and sent him beyond the point of return. He sank deep and she was tight and hot and wet and he knew nothing else because much more basic instincts had taken over by then. His hands gripping her hips, he plunged right into the heated core of her with a shout of shuddering satisfaction. The slap of his flesh against hers joined with the sound of her sobbing breaths and helpless cries. He pushed her legs over his shoulders and drove hard into her tight sheath. She shuddered, feeling the gathering surge of excitement coalesce inside her again as he upped his tempo. It was all too much for her and as he slammed into her one last time she felt the hot blast of his release. Bucking wildly under him, her hips writhed as he thrust her into an indescribably powerful orgasm.

Afterwards the silence was so intense that the

sound of her own breathing felt like a roar in her ears. Zarif settled her back down on the bed with care, resisting the urge to hold her close, and sprang off the bed at speed. He was feeling far too much all at once, too many thoughts screaming through his mind. He was shocked, appalled, drowning in guilt and regret. Snatching up his clothing, he began to get dressed.

'So…that's it, is it?' Ella heard herself say limply, hurt winging through her in an enervating surge. 'No cuddling afterwards?'

'It would not alter what we just did,' Zarif breathed curtly, brushing straight his robes with unsteady hands and heading for the doors that opened out onto the stairs down to the courtyard beyond, desperate for some fresh air and clarity of thought.

Ella's body ached: she was sore. Strange how she had never suspected that the first occasion might hurt so much, she acknowledged numbly. So, of course, Zarif had guessed her deepest darkest secret. She had let the cat out of the bag herself. He was shocked. And he wasn't pleased, of course he wasn't. Clearly he had wanted an experienced lover to entertain him for a year, not a first-timer unfit for a repeat encounter or more carnal games.

Zarif came to an abrupt halt by the central fountain, which played its water in the shade of a clump of palm trees. A virgin. Ella had been a virgin and he had taken her with all the finesse of a rutting beast and naturally he had hurt her. He recalled how careful he had been as a newly married teenager with Azel in spite of his colossal ignorance and he recoiled in disgust at his lack of control with Ella. He had hurt her, wronged her… Was there to be no end to the mistakes he made with her?

In public life, Zarif had made very few mistakes. He was highly intelligent and naturally cautious and he had learned early how to think ahead and protect himself from missteps. A king couldn't expect second chances, a king needed the support of his subjects and had to stay in touch with their prevailing mood to retain the right to rule. He knew for a fact in that instant that he was a better king than he was a husband.

But then, in truth, he had not been fit to touch an innocent woman in the first place and that inescapable awareness tormented him. She had stayed pure in a much more liberal culture than his own, setting a standard he had strikingly failed to follow. For so long he had blamed her for that reality because it had been her rejection that had sent him careening off the rails of restraint. Unbearable as it was to acknowledge, he had been weak where she had been strong. Shame drenched him like perspiration in the heat. He had tried to bring her down to his level by treating her like a sex object and he had failed. But why had she refused to take advantage of the escape clause he had offered her?

Ironically, he had never understood Ella and was indeed beginning to suspect that she was a complete and utter mystery to him. Yet he had often assumed that he *did* understand her and just as often read her entirely wrong, only to discover too late that he had made yet another miscalculation.

She seemed so deceptively open, he acknowledgedly broodingly. He had believed she was playing games with him three years earlier when she said no to his proposal. He had believed she wanted him to propose purely to relish the narcissistic charge of her power over him. Now he doubted that hypothesis and found it quite a challenge to fit an innocent young woman into such a scenario. Perhaps she had said no to marrying him for the very reasons she had stated…the same reasons he had arrogantly dismissed as offensive red herrings. Perhaps she had genuinely *feared* having to adapt to a culture and royal expectations so far removed from her own experience and he had said and done nothing to soothe her concerns.

But why was he looking back to the past when he had created so many more problems here in the present? He had essentially forced her to marry him and forced her into his bed because, loving her parents as she did, she had not had a choice. Possibly that was also why she had urged him to continue in bed, believing as she must have done that sooner or later she *had* to surrender her body to his to meet the terms he had demanded.

Zarif swore below his breath, recognising how complicated everything had become and knowing he had brought it down on himself with no help from anyone else. But then guilt had, for so long, been Zarif's constant companion in life that he almost welcomed it back like an old friend. He was in the wrong. Once again he was in the wrong.

A hundred years ago, one of his ancestors would have dealt much more easily with such a situation, he reflected with sardonic humour. He would have kidnapped her, offered her family handsome compensation for the loss of her and hidden her in the harem, eventually offering her marriage as a reward for her acceptance. It would not have been considered dishonourable. That approach would have dealt practically with a man's need for a woman he could not otherwise have. Zarif knew that his contemporary solution had crashed and burned at spectacular speed, particularly when all he could think about *in spite* of all that had gone wrong was climbing back into that bed with Ella again and proving that in some fields he *could* get it right.

* * *

Ella lowered her body into the bath of warm water and hugged her knees. Well, it was done, she had met the conditions of their agreement and he had no reasonable grounds for complaint now. Seemingly he had not enjoyed the sex as much as he had thought he would, but that was the essential flaw in male fantasy, Ella thought grimly. Fantasy wasn't *real*. He'd had a fantasy about what she would be like and she had failed to live up to it, which wasn't really surprising when one considered that she was simply an ordinary young woman and neither stunningly beautiful nor amazingly sexy.

The bedroom was filled with flowers when she finally emerged from a long soothing bath, wrapped in a towelling robe. Innumerable baskets of white roses sat on every surface and she frowned. Someone knocked on the door and she opened it. An envelope and a gift box were extended to her by a maid.

The envelope contained a plain white card. 'Forgive me,' it said and she compressed her lips into a rigid line. She would have been more inclined towards forgiveness had Zarif stayed around in the flesh to *be* forgiven. She unwrapped the jewellery box and flipped it open on a breathtaking bracelet shaped like a glittering white river of diamonds. She detached it, fastened it round her wrist and rolled her eyes at the extravagance of his apology. She was very much aware that everything Zarif and she herself did was the focus of all too many watchful eyes and wagging tongues amongst the palace staff. People would know he had given her a gift and she had to wear it.

The maid reappeared and opened the closets in the dressing room to withdraw a selection of outfits. Ella stared in surprise at the unfamiliar and obviously brand-new items sheathed in garment bags. Clearly they were for her. She pulled out her phone and called Zarif.

'Did you buy me clothes?' she asked bluntly.

'Ella…how are you?' Zarif enquired smoothly.

'The clothes?' she prompted impatiently.

'Yes. I asked my mother, who is very much involved with the fashion world, to choose a new wardrobe for you.'

'Your mother?' Ella repeated, disconcerted, for the older woman had not even been present at their wedding the day before.

'I assure you that she was happy to be of assistance.'

'But I don't need anything. I have my own clothes.'

'I doubt very much that your present wardrobe will meet the standard of quality and formality which will now be required from you as my queen,' Zarif informed her wryly.

Wandering round the spacious suite of rooms as she talked on the phone, Ella stiffened. 'Is that so?'

'I did not intend to offend you. I merely spoke the truth.'

Ella's vexed gaze fell on a silver-framed photo sited on a corner table in the dining room where they had had breakfast at the start of the day. She stared in dismay at the photo of an attractive brunette with beautiful almond-shaped dark eyes smiling into the camera as she held her equally dark-eyed son.

'Thank you for the flowers, the clothes and the

bracelet,' Ella said woodenly, still gaping at the photo of what could only be her predecessor.

'I should have stayed to speak to you.'

'No, saying it with flowers was better,' Ella broke in. 'We really don't have much to say to each other.'

Not giving him the chance to respond, she tossed the phone down and lifted the photo of Azel and her infant son, Firas. Of course he kept a picture of his late wife and child in his private suite and why wouldn't he? It was a perfectly normal thing to do. He wouldn't want to forget them and he would want to show respect: of course, he had retained a photograph and she couldn't begrudge him that. But she knew the image would very likely haunt her. Zarif's first wife, and cousin, had been an undeniable beauty and the baby was downright adorable but rather too young to be showing any resemblance to his parents in his indeterminate features. Ella returned the portrait to its place, deciding there and then that she didn't want to share living space with Zarif in what was still Azel's place.

There was no reason why she and Zarif should

share a bedroom, she reasoned feverishly. Good grief, had he taken her to the very same bed he had once shared with Azel? She swallowed hard, scanning the decoration of the rooms suspiciously and feeling very much like an intruder. Naturally she would neither ask nor expect him to put the photo away. At the same time, though it possibly wasn't very nice or sympathetic, she worried immediately why she was so determined not to live daily with that reminder of Azel or inhabit the same rooms.

Smartly garbed in a tailored cotton dress, Ella went off to explore and soon discovered that there were so many rooms available that she could probably choose a different one for every night of the year she was to spend in Vashir. She picked a set of interconnecting rooms on the other side of the corridor and was engaged in removing her new clothes from the dressing room when Hanya joined her.

'You are packing to go somewhere?' the tiny brunette asked in surprise.

Ella studied Hanya for a split second, recalling the misunderstanding about how much vodka she had drunk and she still forced a smile. In the future she would watch out for Hanya but for as long as she was forced to consult the other woman as an interpreter and for advice, it would be wiser not to make an enemy of her. 'Just across the corridor. I like my own space and Zarif likes his,' she said lightly.

Hanya called for two maids and, without Ella having to say a word more, she and her belongings, old and new, were resettled across the corridor.

'Queen Azel planned to turn this suite into a nursery because it had more space,' Hanya confided. 'So sad. I expect had my cousin survived she would have been the mother of several children by now.'

'Yes.' Ella refused to let the gloss be stolen from her new accommodation by the news that Azel had hoped to site a nursery there.

'My uncle and the King were inconsolable.' Hanya sighed. 'I wept most for the baby. He was so little and cute.'

'Yes,' Ella responded a little gruffly, finding her own vocal cords tightening when she thought of that tiny face in the photo, a life taken before it even got properly going.

'Azel was much older than I was and because of that we weren't close,' the other woman admitted honestly. 'But we all knew how much she adored the King. For a long time he was lost without her.'

'It was a huge loss,' Ella conceded and then she quite deliberately busied herself putting away her toiletries in the cupboard in the spacious bathroom. In the same bag she came on her contraceptive pills and realised that she had missed one the day before. She took another and hoped that her having missed one would make no difference. She vaguely recalled being told something about having to try and take it at the same time every day and she shook her head ruefully. Two weddings in forty-eight hours and an apparent allergy to shellfish had destroyed her usual routine.

Around ten, Ella went to bed. She had dined with Hanya after Zarif phoned her to tell her that he wouldn't be back until late. She wondered if newly marrieds usually went straight back to work after the wedding in Vashir. Certainly, Zarif did not seem to be acknowledging any need to change his schedule to accommodate a wife. But then why would he? she asked herself irritably. Zarif was well aware that she wasn't a proper wife and that within a year she would be gone, so, even if it was boring and lonely for Ella, it made sense that he should see no point in altering his usual habits.

Just as Ella was contemplating reaching out to douse the bedside light her bedroom door swung open without warning. Startled, she sat up.

Zarif stood poised in the doorway, breathing heavily, his spectacular cheekbones scored with colour. 'What are you doing in here?' he demanded.

'Is there some reason why I shouldn't sleep in another room?' Ella asked shortly, colliding with the fiery golden eyes pinned to her and challenging that look.

'You're my wife. I want you in my bed.'

Ella was astonished by his attitude. 'Surely you can visit me here?'

'But I do not want to *visit*,' Zarif derided with savage distaste, stalking to the bed, thrusting the sheet back with impatient hands and snatching her up off the mattress without ceremony. 'I want you where I know I can find you twenty-four-seven.'

CHAPTER EIGHT

ZARIF TUMBLED HER down on his four-poster bed like a stolen parcel he had forcibly retrieved. Ella sat up, honey-blonde hair fanning round her flushed face, sapphire eyes very bright. 'What are you playing at?'

'This is not a game,' Zarif told her sternly. 'Why did you move out of here?'

Ella stilled. 'I saw Azel's photo in the dining room—at least I assume it was her—and suddenly being here didn't feel comfortable. This is where you lived with her.'

Zarif was rigid with tension, as he always seemed to be when she made any reference to his first wife or child. 'No, it wasn't. We didn't live together in the Western sense.'

Her brow furrowed. 'I don't understand.'

'My grandparents lived together, sharing the same rooms and mealtimes. That was *their* way.

My uncle Halim and his wife, Azel's parents, were more traditional and preferred separate accommodation. Azel was accustomed to that lifestyle and this building has so much unused space that it was not a problem,' he explained flatly. 'Try to remember that we were only teenagers when we married and Azel wanted her own suite where she could entertain her friends and occasionally forget that she was a queen. I doubt if she ever set foot in here.'

Ella was very much surprised by that snapshot of a marriage she had blithely assumed to be a love's young dream of constant togetherness and suddenly she was unable to meet his direct gaze. Had she simply fled from the threat of a photograph? Was she still that over-sensitive about Azel's unassailable position in his heart? And why was that, when she no longer loved him? She didn't love him, had no excuse to feel jealous or possessive about a part of his past that had been written long before she even met him. What was the matter with her?

'The presence of the photo offended you?' Zarif pressed.

'No, of course not.' Ella studied her linked hands with fixed attention. Offended did not describe her feelings. She had felt irrationally *threatened* and *hurt* but that was not for sharing.

'You're still wearing the bracelet,' he said in surprise.

Ella clamped a rueful hand over the glittering diamonds and went pink. 'I couldn't get the clasp undone.'

'Let me…' His dark head lowered, his luxuriant black hair almost brushing her cheek and the exotic scent of sultry spice and earthy male assailed her nostrils. Deft fingers unfastened the tricky clasp and set the bracelet onto the cabinet by the bed. 'I was with my uncle all evening. I didn't intend to leave you alone for so long.'

'That's OK,' Ella said breathlessly as a cell phone buzzed in the tense silence.

Zarif stepped back from the bed to answer his phone. 'I'm sorry, I must take this…'

Talking in Arabic and already, she sensed, mental miles from her, Zarif wandered fluidly across the room and eventually into the room next door. Ella slumped back against the pillows to await his return. It shouldn't matter to him where she chose to sleep. Why was he suddenly bent on always reminding her that she was his wife? Their marriage was fake, and a temporary fake at that, and to her way of thinking she was not *really* his wife, so why did he feel the need to pretend otherwise? As she listened to Zarif's call continuing and the undeniably soothing sound of his calm, well-modulated drawl she smothered a yawn and finally slid out of bed, closed the interconnecting door quietly and switched out the lights.

She had no idea what time it was when she was wakened by an arm tugging her back into contact with a hot, damp, very masculine body. 'Oh!' she gasped, flinching.

'I'm sorry…I didn't intend to wake you,' Zarif breathed.

'Then you shouldn't have put your arm round me…*and* you're damp!' Ella complained loudly before she could think better of it because he immediately whipped his arm off her and shifted away from her.

'Fresh from the shower. I'm not used to sharing a bed,' Zarif sighed. 'I kept on bumping into you and I thought that if I held you close, it would be less unsettling.'

Ella felt oddly abandoned by his retreat and she shimmied backwards until their bodies had made contact again. 'There, now you know where I am.'

Zarif's core temperature was so much hotter than her own that her spine felt burned by the connection, or possibly the real problem was the overheated tingles of awareness that immediately coursed through her when she felt the hard thrust of his erection against her hip. She tensed, insanely aware of the swelling of her breasts and the melting liquid sensation in her pelvis.

'Ignore it…it's just the normal male reaction to being close to a beautiful woman,' Zarif informed her deflatingly.

'I do know that much about men!' Ella shot back, her cheeks warm in the moonlight filtering through the drapes.

'And of course, I've thought of little else all day but the sheer joy of being inside you, *habibti*,' Zarif confessed in a roughened undertone. 'That doesn't help. Even the knowledge that you did not experience the same pleasure doesn't cool my enthusiasm.'

'But I did…at the end,' Ella whispered back, cheeks hotter than ever.

'If only you had told me beforehand that I would be the first,' Zarif groaned into her hair, his arm closing round her to pull her even closer, long finger smoothing across her shoulder. 'Had I known, I would have been much more patient and infinitely more careful to prepare you. It might still have hurt but probably not as much.'

'I didn't *want* you to know,' Ella admitted.

'But why not? It was a gift I never thought to have from you. You should've been proud of your innocence,' he countered in a tone of rebuke. 'But then I should never have just assumed that you had had other lovers.'

'But wasn't that part of your fantasy? That I would be an experienced partner?' Ella prompted tight-mouthed.

'There *was* no fantasy,' Zarif protested heatedly. 'I wanted you so much I didn't care whether you had a past or not. I am not a narrow-minded man.'

'I'm not sure I can believe you…' Ella hesitated

but then she *had* to ask, 'Was it really sheer joy for you?'

'It was amazing for me but the fact that it wasn't for you only made me feel worse,' he growled with grudging honesty.

'It wasn't only the end I enjoyed,' Ella confided.

'No?' Zarif eased his hands below the hem of her camisole top and cupped her breasts, catching the swelling sensitive nipples between his fingers and tugging gently to send curls of molten lust travelling straight to her core. Her hips squirmed, a small explosion of air dragged from between her lips.

'It was only that few s-seconds I didn't enjoy,' she stammered as he began to pull the camisole up and over her head, baring her breasts for his caresses.

'Will you give me another chance to prove myself?' Zarif murmured hungrily in her ear, pausing to nip at the tender slope of skin between her neck and her shoulder with his strong white teeth.

Jerking with a stifled gasp, Ella laughed. 'Now would be a good time.'

Zarif tugged up her legs to extract her from her

shorts. 'If you had said no, go to sleep, I do believe I would have killed you,' he confided with raw amusement. 'I ache for you, *habibti*.'

Ella was aching too and there was an overflowing sensation inside her in the region of her chest, emotions rolling about in wild disarray and, although she couldn't distinguish them, she knew she was on a high and vulnerable. It was just sex, *only* sex, she bargained wildly with herself; there was no need to make it more than it was and little point in punishing herself for meeting the terms of a bargain she had agreed to make. He flipped her round in his arms to kiss her before she could get any further with the sensible talking-to she was giving herself and that single kiss sent every rational thought flying into nothingness. Her hand came up and speared into his thick black hair to hold him to her and the flicker of his tongue inside her mouth filled her with wild hunger.

She twisted against him, squirming, needing, in a way she had never known before. The swollen petals of flesh between her quivering thighs throbbed and when he came over her, she was more than ready for the long hard glide of his sex into hers. Delicious ripples of response fluttered within her. As he rose over her she had a vision of him soaring above the flames during the sword dance and her heart thumped out a wild tattoo.

He shifted his hips, finding another angle, and thrust into her receptive flesh. Plunged into raw excitement, she sobbed with pleasure. Every skin cell was primed to want more as she arched up to him like a cat and locked her legs round his lean hips. Need exploded in her, voracious and impatient, driving her on as she rose to meet his every thrust, helplessly reaching for the climax and revelling in the great starburst of release when it swept over her, raining down a cascade of intense pleasure that relaxed every bone in her body.

'You are delicious, *habibti*,' Zarif husked into the coconut-scented depths of her hair as he eased her onto her side to release her from his weight and kissed her shoulder. 'Utterly delicious.'

Ella roused herself from her slump, surprised that she was still in the circle of his arms. 'You're holding me.'

'Yes…' Zarif breathed without any expression at all.

'This morning you said it would be inappropriate.'

'This morning I felt very much in the wrong for taking advantage of an innocent.'

'But that's not how it was,' Ella countered squarely. 'I knew what I was doing.'

'What is done is done. But on reflection, I see no reason why we should not be together as long as we treat each other with respect and honesty,' Zarif framed stubbornly, ramming down every misgiving, long fingers smoothing the impossibly soft skin of her slender waist while he drank in the scent of her. It was so many years since he had spent an entire night in bed with a woman. He had never slept with his lovers and even Azel had only been an occasional overnight visitor but the idea of returning to find Ella in his bed every night was amazingly appealing…although he could never afford to forget that she was a supreme indulgence that came with time limits.

'So you show respect and apologise by giving me clothes, flowers and a diamond bracelet,' Ella remarked gingerly. 'Don't you know any other way to show care or concern with a woman? Do you always just *buy* things?'

Zarif was stunned by the question, which cut right to the heart of his previous dealings with women. Yes, sadly he *did* just buy things. To say sorry for a cancellation, to express sympathy for a loss or dismissal, to say thank you for an especially good night.

In the silence, Ella gulped. 'It just makes a girl feel a little cheap…that's all,' she told him abstractedly, her voice dwindling because she did not want to start an argument.

'I have had very few…what you might term relationships,' Zarif admitted grittily. 'I am not trying to buy you. Why would I when I have already bought you?'

Stinging tears of painful surprise washed the backs of Ella's eyes. She pulled away from him and turned defensively onto her side. She had spoken without thinking, foolishly forgetting how she had ended up married to him. But how could she have forgotten? How could she have forgotten for one moment how big a part his fabulous wealth had played in their relationship? Without that wealth, without her parents' need for security, she would not be with him now.

'You didn't buy me outright,' she contradicted in a small, tight voice. 'You bought a year-long lease. That's not the same.'

In the dimness, Zarif suddenly grinned with sheer appreciation. He loved that distinction that she brandished like a weapon, refusing to grant him full ownership. *A year-long lease?* Only Ella could have come up with that qualifier.

'And of course we both know that you won't be extending the lease at any stage,' Ella completed thinly, and swallowed hard before adding, 'You know, if this is us being respectful and honest with each other, Zarif, you can keep it! We're just tearing everything apart.'

Involuntarily, Zarif reached for her. They had both spoken the truth, although admittedly not in a productive manner, but he did, however, have a great reverence for the truth, regardless of how tactless or wounding it might be. Yet a tiny, tiny hint of a sniff from the far side of the bed sent him flying across it before he could think better of his behaviour and he tugged her small rigid body back across the divide into his arms.

'Nothing has been torn apart. You are still the same woman. You gave up your freedom for your parents' benefit. How can I not respect such strength and loyalty?' he demanded.

Ella breathed in so deep she was surprised she didn't swell up like a balloon and float away. Some of her rigidity eased and she allowed her body to bend into the heat and solidity of his. 'You really mean that?' she checked.

'I do.'

'By the way, if you decide you want to buy me something…you could make it something small and cheap,' she told him impulsively. 'You know, like the silver pendant and bracelet you bought me for my twenty-first birthday?'

Zarif almost laughed out loud but he held it back. Presumably she had never had that first gift of his valued nor had she studied its marks. The pendant and the bracelet were *not* silver, they were platinum and designed by one of the most famous jewellery designers alive. Although at the time he had not wanted to give her a gift that attracted attention by being too excessive, his desire for her had been so powerful that a small, cheap gift could never have matched what he then believed she was worth. 'Do you still have it?' he asked curiously.

'Yes, that set is still one of my favourite pieces,' she muttered sleepily.

Ella wakened still wrapped in Zarif's arms. 'What time is it?' she whispered.

'Almost six. I have to get up soon but you can lie as long as you like,' he breathed lazily, sliding against her, the hard thrust of his intentions obvious to her even in her drowsy state.

Heat burned low in her body and she couldn't believe it after the night they had shared. 'I need a shower,' she told him uncomfortably.

'No, you smell of me and a long adventurous night of loving and you wouldn't believe how hot I find that, *habibti,*' he husked, long fingers rubbing at her engorged nipples and sliding lower to tease the most sensitive spot on her entire body. 'You make me insatiable.'

But if that was his flaw, it was one she shared

with him, her head falling back against a broad shoulder as he lifted her thigh and eased into her in a long, slow, gentle glide that left her bereft of breath and protest. Her body stretched to hold him and a piercing sweetness gripped her racing heart at how natural and right it felt to lie with him like that. With subtle erotic movements, he stroked her inner depths with fluid insistence and the pleasure rose and rose and rose until she couldn't contain it any more and it spilled over into bliss as she gasped her excitement into the pillow beneath her.

When she wakened the second time she was alone and hot and she got straight out of bed to stand directly below the whirling fan on the ceiling and flinch at the tenderness that motion wrenched from the long night of loving, as he had called it. Only it wasn't love, she reminded herself, it was just sex. Incredibly good and satis-fying sex, she was willing to admit, but love had nothing to do with it. She showered and break-fasted and dressed, determined to go out and at least see the city rather than pass the day in aim-less pursuits. Zarif had a purpose in life and she needed one as well, even if it was only the role of acting tourist for a year, she reflected ruefully.

Hamid phoned while she was eating to offer her a tour of the palace. She played for time. 'When will Zarif be back?' she asked.

'He will be in meetings with the council most of the day,' his chief aide informed her.

A germ of an idea occurred to Ella. 'And those are like parliament…held in public? I'd like to attend today,' she told Hamid cheerfully. 'Perhaps someone could translate the proceedings for me.'

There was a lengthy period of quiet at the other end of the phone and then Hamid said that he would call her back. Frowning while she wondered if her every move had to be run past Zarif first, Ella ate another piece of croissant.

Zarif was having coffee with his personal staff at the new palace when Hamid phoned him to tell him what his wife wanted to do.

'No woman has crossed the threshold of the council chamber before,' his chief aide pointed out.

'I hope you didn't tell her *that*,' Zarif retorted, thinking of how he had proudly declared that

Vashir was not backward. 'There is no actual rule against female attendance.'

'But it still hasn't happened.'

Lean, darkly handsome features furiously tense, Zarif took his phone into a private room. 'I don't care if you grab women in off the street to attend,' he admitted tautly. 'My wife will attend but I don't want her to be the *only* female present. And I very definitely do *not* want her to realise that, until now, only men have come to observe how the ruling council works. She will think we are very old-fashioned and that our women are not politically aware.'

Hamid thought of his wife, who was a radical with equally radical friends, and knew exactly who to call. He came off the phone, stunned by his royal employer's assent to breaking a tradition that had held firm for at least two hundred years.

'This queen is going to make a difference!' his wife carolled jubilantly. 'Just like the King's British grandmother—she's going to be an innovator and drag this wretched country out of the ark.'

Gloriously unaware of the hopes she was raising with her simple request, Ella selected a dark-coloured outfit with a jacket from her new wardrobe, reasoning that such a visit was formal. Hanya came hurrying down into the palace foyer to join her as she awaited the limo drawing up outside.

'I had no idea you had such plans. My cousin, Azel, would never have dreamt of entering the council chambers,' she exclaimed, giving Hamid a look of reproof as if Ella's wilfulness and unwomanly interest were to be laid at his door. 'Azel said it was the men's place.'

Ella gave the excitable brunette a tranquil smile. 'The machinery of government is not wholly the province of men where I come from. I'm simply interested to see how the council works.'

The new palace was a massive domed building surrounded by a park composed of trees, fountains and walkways and it was extremely busy. Ella only became aware of the half-dozen palace guards accompanying her when they climbed out of the cars that had travelled in front and behind the limo. Feeling uncomfortably conspicuous and colouring from the intensity of the attention she was attracting, she was even more embarrassed when two of the soldiers stationed at the front entrance insisted on leading the way and clearing every other unfortunate out of her path. The buzz of comment around her grew louder and many phones were used to take photos.

'Why's there such a fuss about me coming here?' she asked Hamid.

'I have no idea, Your Majesty,' Hamid lied dutifully for his royal boss. 'But you must remember that apart from the official photo taken at the airport and published in the evening paper very few people have actually seen you and naturally they are curious.'

It was a relief for Ella to leave the busy halls and corridors to ascend the stairs into the main council chamber. A gaggle of chattering women sat to the far left and she naturally moved in that direction as the men present craned their necks and then suddenly shot up and began to bow. An absolute hush fell and seconds later Ella was silenced as the dozen or so old men seated round the large table in the centre of the room also rose to their feet and ceremoniously bowed in her direction. Her colour high, she was trying to spot Zarif but couldn't see him.

Thirty seconds later, he arrived through another door and the whole bowing and scraping thing happened again for his benefit. Ella would have followed suit had not Hamid rested an apologetic hand on her arm as he stood and told her, 'You are the only person in the room who need not rise. It was a courtesy extended by the King's grandfather to his British wife and will also be extended to you. Before the King's grandfather married, Vashiri subjects used to kneel and touch their forehead to the floor in the royal presence, so bowing was also a big step forward...'

Taken aback by the information of how servile the response to royalty had once been, Ella nodded while abstractedly watching Zarif and smiling. He was the only man at the table wearing a business suit and he wore it to perfection. A man so old and wizened he bore a definite resemblance to an Egyptian mummy began to speak about a boundary dispute with a neighbouring country and recommended a heavily armed squad of Vashiri troops be sent to the area.

Hamid translated fluently. Zarif spoke well and suggested that diplomacy be employed before the army became involved.

'The sheikhs will not argue with the King when it comes to military matters because he was once a soldier and the army would follow him into hell, so there's no point in them interfering,' Hamid assured her. 'But only in that field does your husband get a free pass.'

And so it transpired as Ella watched and listened to the discussion of various questions on the agenda, ranging from how best to deal with drunken tourists in Qurzah to the troublesome matter of the royal museum in the new palace, which was still not officially open after months of preparation. Zarif's patience was astounding. There were several petty objections from the council, several of whom appeared to be of the opinion that allowing any private information about the royal family into the public domain even in the educational guise of a museum was unwise. Ella guiltily swallowed back a yawn because she was finding it very tiring to concentrate on the flow of constant translation in her ear.

'Your husband takes a break in a private room for lunch,' Hamid informed her. 'He has asked that you join him there.'

Ella nodded and quietly stood up. Hamid asked if he might introduce his wife, Soraya, to her and signalled with his hand towards the group of women on the other side of the room. An elegant brunette with upswept hair and a bright smile moved forward and introductions were performed. Soraya was on the PR committee for the royal museum and, while frustrated by the fact that the project was moving so slowly, she was very much a working woman, plainspoken and direct in her manner, unlike Hanya. They chatted for a couple of minutes before Hamid intervened and swept Ella off.

'This is a surprise, *habibti*,' Zarif murmured with a slow-burning smile when Ella entered the room.

It had been so long since Zarif looked at her like that that Ella was momentarily thrown back in time. The forbidding aspect of his lean, strong features was washed away by the warmth and welcome of that smile and it flipped her heart inside her chest and shortened her breathing.

'You suit dark blue,' he remarked while the meal was being brought to the table, his attention ranging over the contrast of the honey-coloured skeins of her hair against the backdrop of the comparatively dismal colour. He had once thought blue eyes were dull and ordinary but the brilliant blueness of Ella's gaze against her smooth pale skin never failed to attract his attention.

'You can thank your mother's wonderful taste,' Ella said, and paused before she decided to just come right out and ask what politeness had urged her to suppress since the wedding. 'Why didn't your mother return to Vashir for our wedding or even come over for the UK one?'

Zarif's mouth took on a sardonic twist. 'Mariyah has lived abroad since my birth and has never played a role in my life.'

Ella was taken aback by that admission. 'Why not?'

'What are the two most important facts you need to know about the al-Rastani dynasty? One, we have always been a family with very few male heirs and, two, it has always been the ruler's right to *choose* his successor,' Zarif explained wryly. 'My grandfather, Karim, had one son, Halim, and my mother was his only other child. When my uncle Halim was still quite young, his father decided that he was not suited to being a ruler—Halim does not perform well in a crisis.'

'That must have been a devastating blow for Halim,' Ella remarked with sympathy.

'My uncle very much prefers his books and considered the life he led while Regent during my minority unpleasant and stressful,' Zarif advanced ruefully.

'You were telling me about your mother before I interrupted you.'

'Halim's wife gave birth only to daughters and, consequently, the lack of a male heir to the throne became a crisis. That was when my grandfather asked my mother to marry and provide the remedy.'

Ella pulled a face as she casually picked at her lamb and rice casserole with a fork. 'And you were the remedy,' she guessed.

'But not an easy remedy from my unfortunate mother's point of view,' Zarif declared grimly. 'She married an obnoxious playboy with a proven history of fathering male sons purely because she knew that all he was interested in was her money and that he would never seek to interfere with her life or mine.'

'You're referring to Gaetano Ravelli, who's Nik and Cristo's father as well?' Ella prompted. '*Was* he obnoxious?'

'Without a doubt, he was a very selfish, dissolute man. I actually never met him. He had no interest in his children.'

'I know that Belle and Cristo are raising his children by Belle's mother, who was his mistress for years,' Ella admitted. 'But I really know nothing else about him. Did your mother hold your genes against you? Are you estranged because you remind her of Gaetano?'

'We're not estranged, but we are basically still strangers,' Zarif admitted, his dark golden eyes unusually sombre. 'She handed me over at birth to her parents to raise and when my grandparents died, Halim took over. Mariyah knew that I would never fully be *her* child because my grandfather planned to make me his heir and would insist on overseeing every aspect of my upbringing. Karim ensured that I attended a military school, went straight into the army and that I married Azel. After my mother divorced Gaetano she asked my grandfather's permission to live abroad. She has lived in Italy ever since and the only visits she has ever made back to Vashir were to honour my grandparents' passing and to see Halim, shortly after his terminal illness was diagnosed.'

'Have you ever actually *tried* to connect with her?' Ella prompted.

'Not in the sense that you mean. Although when I approached Mariyah for help with your wardrobe it was because I knew she would enjoy the challenge…and perhaps I wanted to make her feel a part of my life, even if it was only in a small way.' Zarif shrugged broad shoulders and sighed in frustration, spelling out the reality that he hated to talk about emotional things. 'But as people, what would my mother and I have in common now? Although my mother was born royal she hated the restrictions and sacrifices that being royal forced on her. She refuses to even use her title. She forged a successful career as a fashion stylist in the film world and enjoys the freedom of her anonymity.'

'I still think it's sad that you have no contact.' Ella was thinking unhappily of him growing up without a mother while wondering if his grandparents had been loving replacements or more concerned about guaranteeing that they raised the most suitable possible royal heir to the throne. Military school, the army and a very youthful marriage to a chosen bride, the cousin he had grown up with. Such a rigidly conformist background did not suggest to her that Zarif had been allowed much licence to develop as an individual in his own right. From an early age, he had been denied the freedom to choose that which other people took for granted. She believed that the presence of a protective mother might have ensured he had more fair and liberal choices.

'My life is what it is and my mother and I inhabit different worlds,' Zarif retorted wryly.

Her cell phone pinged with a message and she

pulled it out because her mother had been seeing her heart specialist that morning and had promised to relay her latest test results. But the name that popped up on the screen was Jason's and she put the phone back in her bag because she was in no hurry to read what her brother might have to say. Doubtless it would be another boastful text about wildly entertaining drunken parties or the ludicrously dangerous ski runs that he loved to do.

'I'm afraid I have to get back to work again,' Zarif revealed. 'Are you staying on for the second session?'

'No, I think I'll go and do a bit of shopping this afternoon.' Ella drained her glass of water and slowly stood. 'So, you're going back to deal with the old fossils, are you?'

Zarif's brilliant dark gaze glittered with wicked appreciation. 'I try to be a democrat.' He reached for her hands and pulled her close, his thumbs massaging her fragile wrist bones. 'I'm dining with you tonight.'

Her pink-tinted mouth pouted as she looked up at him. 'To what do I owe the honour?'

'You want an honest answer?' As she nodded, Zarif laughed. 'Your show of interest in government. Until today no woman had ever set foot in the council chamber and my uncle is so shocked by news of your interest that he suggested I am leaving you alone too much!'

Her eyes widened and then glimmered with matching amusement. 'And you said Vashir wasn't backward?' she teased.

'I lied. I wanted you to love it here as much as I do and I didn't want to line up all the flaws for your edification at your very first viewing.'

His mouth settled down over hers and her lush lips clung to his with a sudden fervour she could not restrain, hunger winging through her slender body in a wave she could not suppress. Zarif yanked his proud dark head back up, studying her with raw heat in his burning gaze. 'Later,' he husked sexily.

'Hold on a minute!' Ella exclaimed, digging into her bag with a tissue and stretching up on tiptoe to wipe the stain of pink from his wide, sensual mouth. 'The King can't be seen in public smeared with lipstick.'

Ella was still smiling without knowing what she was smiling about when she climbed into the limousine. She thrust the stained tissue back in her bag and then remembered Jason's text. With a rueful look in her eyes, she dug out her phone to read her brother's message.

RUNNING OUT OF MONEY. NEED A CASH IN-JECTION… 100,000 WOULD TIDE ME OVER.

Ella studied Jason's demand with wide, discom-fited eyes and her mouth tightened. Jason really did have no shame. She texted back in haste.

I WILL NOT ASK ZARIF FOR MONEY FOR YOU.

HE'D BETTER PAY UP IF HE DOESN'T WANT HIS MISTRESSES IN DUBAI REVEALED TO THE MEDIA.

Hollow with shock and horror, Ella sat trans-fixed, staring at the screen of her phone. They were driving through the city centre by the time she got a grip on her roiling emotions. She lifted the phone to communicate with Hamid, who was seated beside the driver. 'I want to return to the old palace. I'm too tired to go shopping this afternoon,' she announced.

Mistresses? In Dubai? Her tummy dropped to the soles of her feet and her facial bones were clenched so tightly that her face felt frozen. Was it true? Was Zarif entertaining multiple women in his bed, just as his ancestors had done in the days of the harem?

CHAPTER NINE

ELLA AGONISED FOR what remained of the afternoon over the thorny question of whether or not she had the right to ask Zarif awkward questions.

It was a matter of decency, she told herself. She wasn't prepared to have sex with a male who might still intend to engage in encounters with other women at the first opportunity. The sick feeling in her stomach was disgust at that suspicion, nothing more personal. She was not hurt or jealous. To experience either reaction, she would have to be in love with Zarif and only the most stupid woman in the world would have fallen in love with a man who only wanted her body in his bed for a year. And she was, most assuredly, not stupid. Zarif had never had deeper feelings for her and what you didn't have, you could hardly miss. In fact, a sexual affair conducted on the lines of the utmost practicality and honesty was much less dangerous than one wrapped in honeyed lies and pretences.

Thus bolstered by a fine head of superior steam interlaced with deep abiding shame at her brother's threats, Ella sat down to dinner with Zarif and simply placed her phone in front of him, opened up so that Jason's texts could easily be read. 'You said we should be honest with each other, so I thought you should see this.'

In smouldering silence, Zarif studied the screen, beautiful wilful mouth twisting with derision, but Ella also noticed the hint of pallor that had paled his golden skin and the tension that steadily entered his big powerful frame.

'I will deal with this. Don't respond,' he instructed smoothly. 'But I think Jason will find it a great challenge to sell another story about either of us. My legal team has already demonstrated my zeal with regard to protecting your reputation in the British courts this week. The tabloid that printed that sleazy article on our wedding day will be printing a retraction and I am suing them for millions.'

Ella stuffed a lettuce leaf into her dry mouth

and waited but that, it seemed, was that. Zarif mentioned how unexpectedly well Halim was doing on his new drug treatment and informed her that he had decided to extend their current accommodation into the suites on either side to give them more space. He then told her with a warm smile of amusement that her appearance in the council chambers that morning had made the headlines in the evening paper.

Indeed they had reached the dessert course of fresh fruit and cheese when Ella mastered her growing incredulity at his shocking ability to avoid the obvious and said dulcetly, 'And that's it? You've said all you intend to say about Jason's allegations?'

Dark golden eyes set with stunning effect below winged ebony brows and a lush cloak of blacker than black lashes gazed in serene challenge back at her. 'I answer to no one on the score of my private life,' he declared smooth as velvet.

Temper bubbled up through Ella's stiffening frame. 'You answer to me!' she contradicted without hesitation.

'And why would you assume that?' Zarif enquired in the mildest of tones, his handsome features taut with proud assurance and steadfast cool.

Ella thrust back her chair and stood up, her eyes electric blue with steadily mounting rage. 'Because you married me.'

'But it is not a conventional marriage. It is more one of convenience for both of us.'

Ella whirled round to face him so fast that her hair slapped against her cheeks. 'I will not sleep with a man who is planning to sleep with other women!'

Zarif left the table at an infuriatingly leisurely pace and strolled forward. 'Then you have no possible cause for concern. You are presently the only woman in my life or my bed.'

'Couldn't you just have told me that upfront?' Ella almost screeched at him in vexation. 'And ditched the macho need to tell me that I have no right to question your behaviour?'

'My past is none of your business,' Zarif stated on a note of distinct challenge. 'You go beyond your boundaries when you try to question me.'

'Do I indeed?' Ella hurled back, trembling with

rage. 'Then maybe you should've spelt out those boundaries *before* we got married!'

'A clear oversight for which I apologise,' Zarif murmured as smoothly as ever.

'There are times when I *hate* you!' Ella launched at him full volume, her hands clenching into fists of frustration by her side.

'I will not stand here while you shout at me,' Zarif told her grimly, lean, strong face hard as iron as he strode towards the door.

'If you run away sooner than answer my perfectly reasonable questions, I will see it as an act of *extreme* masculine cowardice,' Ella informed him with fiery vehemence.

Temperamentally incapable of ignoring a charge of that magnitude, Zarif froze two steps from the door before swinging almost violently back round to survey her with glittering golden eyes of sheer fury. 'How dare you?'

'I dare because I want answers,' Ella admitted grittily.

'Even if you're not entitled to them?'

'The way I see it, I was entitled to answers the instant we shared a bed,' Ella replied with a toss of her head. 'Do you have an apartment in Dubai?'

Zarif considered the question for several burning seconds and compressed his lips. 'I do. Have I kept women there? I have but it is presently empty,' he concluded curtly.

'And is it going to stay empty for the duration of our marriage?' Ella prompted, more than a little relieved that he had chosen to respond.

'For as long as you are with me,' Zarif confirmed in a low-pitched growl, his brooding rancour over her persistence unhidden in the stubborn set of his jaw line and the angled-back height of his proud dark head.

A touch mollified, Ella nodded. 'But you *did* keep women there?' she could not resist asking, her curiosity thrusting to the fore naked and embarrassing in its strength.

'One at a time,' Zarif divulged, lean, strong face set hard. 'I have needs like any other man. I will not apologise for that.'

Ella studied him with a sinking heart, suddenly feeling very vulnerable. 'Tell me, how did I escape an invite to occupy the apartment in Dubai?'

Zarif vented a harsh laugh. 'I wanted to see more of you—an ambition that is presently ebbing fast.'

Ella felt the bite of that derisive dismissal like a knife piercing her breast. This was her lover talking down to her as if she was nothing, nobody, virtual mud below his royal feet. This was not the respect he had promised her. 'On *both* sides,' she stressed tightly. 'But it's perfectly obvious to me that all I am is your mistress within marriage.'

'If that is true,' Zarif countered with a raw edge to his deep dark drawl, 'then go and wait for me in bed and put on something sexy before you go there because I am in the mood to play and dispel the memory of this distasteful scene.'

'You can go take a running jump into the nearest sand dune!' Ella launched back at him in outraged disbelief.

The door opened on the servants entering to clear the table. Zarif was rigid and the silence smouldered and crackled like an invisible fire. His stunning eyes were a ferocious golden blaze of unashamed fury.

'Or not,' Ella framed, just a little unnerved by

the unholy temper she could see him restraining for she had never, ever seen him lose it.

'A word?' With an imperious signal of one lean brown hand, Zarif virtually ordered her out into the corridor where he lowered his arrogant dark head to say, 'Three years ago I asked you to marry me and you said no. Do not expect to enjoy the same privileges that I would have offered you then,' he advised grimly. 'That time is past.'

He was a bad loser, Ella translated, a little shiver of foreboding travelling down her taut spine. 'I think I liked you better back then.'

'But not enough to marry me.'

You stupid, stupid man, I *loved* you! she almost screamed after him as he strode off, shoulders back, military carriage obvious in every angle of his bearing. She went out to the gardens to walk at a fast pace. She had to do something to expel the billows of rage still shrieking around inside her in need of an exit. The two guards following her down every path taxed her patience as she could not imagine that any possible ill could befall her in a literal fortress surrounded by high walls and enough armed men to fight a war. Her temper under control again, she opted for a long bath and an early night.

She could not stop thinking about the apartment in Dubai where Zarif had clearly been entertained by a steady procession of women. Sexually sophisticated women, who would think nothing of putting on adventurous lingerie to titillate him. Women who probably did exactly what he told them every time because they were eager to please and be rewarded for their obedience. Shallow, superficial affairs, she decided heavily. Yet Zarif, as proven by his deep attachment to his first wife, was capable of so much more.

Only he didn't want *more*, particularly not with Ella, who had once turned him down. He wanted only convenient sex, and her wedding ring simply put a stamp of respectability on the arrangement. In reality, however, she was as much of a whore as the women he had kept in the Dubai apartment, she reflected wretchedly. She might think that she did not have a submissive bone in her body but she had pretty much done exactly as she was told from the minute she agreed to marry him. And why had she agreed? For the cold, hard cash that had put her parents' lives back on the rails. Consequently, she had no right to feel superior in any way to Zarif's mistresses. He had recognised that at heart she was just the same as his other sexual partners and willing to do whatever it took if the reward was great enough, so how could she ask for respect?

Zarif came to bed late and stayed on his own side of the bed while Ella pretended to be asleep. She was ashamed of the facts he had forced her to face and deeply unhappy at the position she had put herself in because she could see no escape hatch. In the morning Zarif was gone and that was the start of a very lonely three weeks during which Ella scarcely saw him. He breakfasted before she got out of bed, which relieved her as during the third week she realised that she seemed to be suffering from a lingering tummy bug, which she blamed on her new diet. She was nauseous several mornings and actually sick on a couple of occasions but was fine the rest of the time.

Unaware of those early morning travails, Zarif

occasionally appeared for lunch, during which time he would make perfectly polite conversation, which chilled her. He went back to dining nightly with Halim. One morning he announced without any self-consciousness that he was flying out to a meeting in Dubai. She lay sleepless in bed that night, wondering if he had betrayed her trust because, while he was not sleeping with her, she did not think she could afford to assume that he would not seek relief with someone else. She kept busy during the days, reading and bathing in the giant deserted swimming pool in the basement that had once housed the harem. She also embarked on lessons in Arabic and wandered aimlessly round the shopping malls, rarely buying anything but frequently photographed.

During the second week, Zarif's uncle came unexpectedly to her rescue by asking her through the medium of Hamid if she would like to preside over the official opening of a new school. Realising that a positive response would be expected of her, she agreed and then fretted about what to say and do at the event until Hamid offered her his wife, Soraya, as an advisor.

Soraya gave her invaluable help. The other woman helped her write a short speech, taught her to say it word perfect in Arabic and even advised her on what to wear. Ella made the visit, inwardly quaking with nerves, but soon relaxed at the friendly response she received and she loved chatting with the children, who wanted to practise their English on her. She managed to smile for the photographers and was feeling both proud and defiant by the time she returned to the old palace.

'You did well today at the school,' Zarif startled her by saying when he was undressing for bed. 'Everyone was impressed.'

The sudden break of his icy reserve disconcerted her. 'I didn't know you were aware of it.'

'Who do you think suggested it to Halim?'

Ella flushed and felt foolish. She watched his silhouette, which was starkly apparent in the moonlight piercing the drapes. As he dropped the towel he wore round his hips she glimpsed the long thick length of his erection and stared before hastily shutting her eyes tight. Perhaps he hadn't had his needs met in Dubai, after all.

But then she hadn't had her needs met either, she thought impatiently, pressing the swollen tenderness of her breasts into the mattress and clamping her thighs tight shut on the ache stirring there.

It was all his wretched fault, Ella decided angrily. She had managed fine without sex until Zarif appeared on her horizon like a battleship bent on a seek-and-destroy mission. Now the scent of his cologne, the memory of their lovemaking or even the sounds he made getting ready for bed lit a fire of treacherous longing in her pelvis. She told herself that it was good to know that he was suffering too and that his self-control was little better than her own. But she still cursed the fact that he had refused to let her occupy a room of her own. And then she thought, Why should he have it all his own way?

In a movement that startled Zarif she flung back the sheet and flipped over to study him. His long, lean, aroused body lay extended for her perusal and the fire inside her leapt higher, a surge of wetness moistening her feminine core. Before she could even think about what she was doing she pressed her mouth to the smooth, muscular expanse of his bronzed stomach. The salty taste of his skin went to her head like wine and the way he jerked in surprise sent a wicked smile of amusement across her mouth.

One hand resting on a hair-roughened thigh, she trailed the tip of her tongue along the length of his bold shaft and felt every muscle in his body snap taut. She traced his hard, velvet-smooth contours with lingering enjoyment, a sense of power flooding her when he laced his fingers into her hair and arched his hips up to her in ready acquiescence. As she sucked him deep he groaned out loud and she wanted to punch the air at finally smashing through the icy deadlock barrier of his reserve. Long fingers caressed her scalp.

Zarif was in shock but incredibly turned on by her unexpected sensual assault. Once or twice he winced when she grazed him with her teeth and then suddenly he smiled triumphantly at her down-bent head, guessing that he was very probably the first man in her life to benefit from her attention. As the intensity rose he gently tugged at her hair. 'No more, *habibti*,' he husked. 'I want to finish inside you…'

A little uncertainly, Ella lifted her head and he sat up so fast and claimed her mouth in a searing kiss that she felt dizzy but unbelievably eager for him to continue.

'I've been such a fool,' Zarif groaned, flattening her to the mattress with more haste than finesse and sliding between her slender thighs with barely contained eagerness. 'I'm too proud, too used to winning every argument. Azel never argued with me, never confronted me.'

'That was bad for you,' Ella breathed on the back of a long dragged-out gasp as he pushed up her hips and plunged into her with a stirring groan of appreciative hunger that she felt down to her toes.

'You're good for me,' Zarif intoned hoarsely, circling his hips to longer enjoy the hot, tight, wet depth of her welcome. He shifted into a series of fast, deep thrusts that drove all prospect of dialogue from her head.

Every mad skip of her heartbeat and every impelling plunge of his possession was breathlessly, insanely exciting. He laboured long and hard over her yearning body and she came in a great pulsating surge of release, his name breaking from her lips as he shuddered over her.

They lay still, wrapped tightly together, both of them struggling for breath.

'You had a right to ask those questions,' he conceded wryly. 'But although I should stop the tasteless comparisons, Azel never asked and I'm not accustomed to full and frank discussions of that nature.'

Stunned by his sudden loquaciousness on the forbidden topic of Azel, Ella lay as still as a mouse facing up to a cat. 'She never asked you if you were faithful to her?'

'She was probably aware that I had been told I didn't have to be faithful when I agreed to marry her. Her parents would have prepared her for that eventuality. They left nothing to chance. We were pawns in a much bigger game. Halim might not have got the throne but his consolation was that his daughter would become my queen.' Zarif sighed.

'Was she ambitious for that status?' Ella whispered.

'No. She genuinely loved me,' Zarif conceded,

rolling back from her to throw himself into a cooler spot on the bed. He stretched out a hand though and enclosed hers. Suddenly the future no longer seemed so threatening and uncertain. The silence stretched and it was a strangely soothing silence. Ella slid slowly into a deep sleep, more relaxed and happier than she had been in weeks.

'You mean, this is not the *first* time?' Zarif exclaimed, unfurling his cell phone to contact Halim's doctor and furious that he had been left out of the loop. 'Why didn't you tell me?'

'Oh, do go away and stop fussing, Zarif,' Ella groaned as she endeavoured to freshen up at the sink after a bout of sickness had sent her careening out of bed straight into the bathroom where the very last thing she had wanted was an audience. 'It's only a little tummy upset…probably the change of diet. I'm eating so much spice.'

'I will hire a British cook if this is the result. How often has this happened?' Zarif demanded, directing a stream of Arabic at the two hovering maids, nodding, compressing his wide sensual mouth as the answers came and confirmed his worst suspicions. His lean, devastatingly handsome face darkened along with his mood.

'You're going back to bed,' Zarif informed Ella, scooping her up and carrying her back into the bedroom where he laid her down with great care.

Ella felt too dizzy and sweaty to argue. Dr Mansour arrived with a nurse, his voice a deep soothing rumble that eventually contrived to make Zarif simmer down. Anyone would be forgiven for thinking that a minor bout of sickness was an emergency, Ella thought ruefully. Some tests were done with her assistance and were quickly followed by an examination.

At the end of it all, Dr Mansour asked the nurse to wait in the other room. A big beaming smile had transformed his guarded expression and the look he spread between Zarif and Ella was warm with appreciation. 'I am deeply honoured to offer my congratulations on this happy event, which will mean so much both to you and to our country…'

'H-happy event?' Ella stammered in bewilderment.

'You have conceived, Your Majesty. You

must've conceived almost immediately after your marriage,' the older man informed her cheerfully. 'Hardly a surprising development for a young and healthy couple but a very welcome one.'

In shock, Ella focused on Zarif, who appeared to be frozen in the centre of the room. She could see the pallor spreading below his bronzed complexion, the skin tightening over his spectacular bone structure. *Pregnant?* How on earth could she be pregnant?

'But I've been taking the contraceptive pill,' Ella protested and named the brand.

'We wanted to wait a few months,' Zarif breathed stiltedly, clearly already engaged in a cover-up because the older man had not been able to hide his surprise that in their circumstances they could have chosen to use contraception rather than try immediately to provide the very much wanted heir to the throne.

The older man smiled wryly. 'Of course but that particular brand, I'm afraid, was not a good choice. It is usually prescribed to regulate a woman's system.'

'Which is what I was taking it for...' Ella's

voice was dwindling away while the great tide of sheer astonishment was rolling over her. A baby... She was going to have a baby, Zarif's baby? Even in that first piercing moment of disbelief, she was aware of the warm tide of acceptance and happiness rising inside her. She might not be able to have him but he couldn't stop her from having his child, she thought helplessly.

'Unfortunately that type of pill has to be taken strictly at the same time every day and it is not reliable if pills are missed or there is an episode of illness, such as you had on your wedding day,' Dr Mansour explained. 'Other precautions would have had to be taken for the rest of that month.'

Ella nodded with all the animation of a marionette and dared not look at Zarif to see how he was reacting to the news that her ignorance of the efficacy of her contraception had contributed to their current predicament. 'Thank you for clarifying that, Doctor.'

The older man lingered to advise her on how best to cope with the morning sickness and recommended an obstetrician in the city, while adding ruefully that it would be unwise to consider conducting the allergy tests he had advised until after she had given birth.

A baby? Zarif was in a daze. He studied Ella's flat stomach and thought of his child growing there and he wanted to touch her so badly at that moment that his hands knotted into fists by his side. Ella had conceived. Had she planned it that way? There could be no surer way of holding onto her status as his wife than by giving him a child.

'You said it was safe,' Zarif reminded her tautly as soon as they were alone.

Ella stared up fixedly at the canopy of the bed above her, guilt slashing through her at the simplicity of that reminder that really said all that needed to be said. He felt he had been deceived. He felt trapped by a development he would actively have guarded against had he known it was possible.

'I honestly *did* think it was safe. When I began taking that pill, it wasn't for contraception and I probably didn't pay a lot of heed to any warnings that were in the instructions. That first day… we were together,' she framed awkwardly, 'I assumed it would be safe because I've been taking it for a couple of years and one's always reading about how very long it can take for a woman to fall pregnant. I mean, I really didn't think it *could* be that easy.'

'Obviously you're very fertile,' Zarif pointed out flatly.

'I couldn't help the fact that I was sick the night before we slept together!' Ella argued, feeling that she had to defend herself. 'It didn't occur to me that I was probably no longer protected because of that. I was convinced that I was telling you the truth when I said it was safe.'

'Were you really?' Zarif queried in a tone she had never heard him use before, a tone of doubt and mistrust. 'Or did you work out for yourself that this is the one development that will ensure I do *not* divorce you and set you aside after a year?'

Ella dealt him an appalled appraisal, shaken that he could think her capable of such manipulative behaviour. 'That's a filthy thing to say. How can you even suspect that?'

'Naturally I'm suspicious…particularly after you threw yourself at me last night. Presumably you didn't yet realise that you were already pregnant and we had not been having sex. Obviously you had to ensure sex took place to have any hope of conceiving.'

'I did not *throw* myself at you!' Ella launched, rearing up in the bed in a positive fury.

Zarif knew he was burning boats but he couldn't stop himself from working up a firestorm in which resentment, incredulity and suspicion dominated. Just at that moment it was too deeply painful for him to think about the baby on the way and the savage irony that for him and Ella conception had happened so very easily. All that he would allow himself to think was that once again he was being forced into a path he had not freely chosen. There were very few things in his life that he was free to choose for himself but this time around, at least, he had had the freedom to choose his own wife. And now that was gone and his little piece of self-indulgence had become a life sentence.

His stormy departure left a terrible silence stretching in its wake. Slowly, carefully, Ella got up, standing only when she was convinced that the sick dizziness had faded. She sat down at the breakfast table and sipped at the special ginger tea Dr Mansour had said he would order from the kitchens for her. She supposed she would have to start thinking of all sorts of things that she had never had to consider before. In fact her every action would have to be tailored to whatever would best suit the baby she carried. A baby, Ella thought, splaying a hand across her flat tummy with quiet and loving satisfaction. Zarif's baby. Yet how could she want the child of a man she hated?

Of course hatred was a little over the top as a description of her feelings, she conceded. Events had suddenly got wildly out of control and Zarif was a dot every 'i' and cross every 't' man, who liked to plan everything. The conception of a child with the wrong woman was a shockingly unexpected development and he hadn't reacted well. Had she supposed he would? Presumably being male he was not being bombarded by the warm, positively fluffy pictures of a cuddly baby currently consuming her thoughts.

CHAPTER TEN

ZARIF SHARED THE news with Halim and Halim was overjoyed and hailed Ella as the most wonderful woman ever. 'So soon...already a little mother-to-be,' he kept on saying, patting his nephew's arm in fond emphasis. 'A gift is in order, a gift to express my great joy and gratitude.'

'It could be a girl,' Zarif pointed out, disconcerted by his uncle's gushing effusions and suddenly painfully aware that his own reaction should have been similar.

'Then the next will be a male.' Halim would not allow anyone to rain on his parade. 'Are you happy, my boy? Or does all this only bring back unhappy memories?'

'A little of both,' Zarif admitted truthfully. 'You will forgive me if I return to Ella now?'

'This is a new beginning for you and our family, Zarif,' the old man told him quietly. 'Don't allow the sadness of the past to shadow the present.'

But the past had made Zarif who he was, honing him down to the essentials of duty and honour and making him a very tough judge of his own behaviour. And now without the smallest warning he was aware of all the many things that he had *not* said to Ella and, desert robes swishing in accompaniment to his long, forceful stride, he sped back to the quarters he shared with his wife.

When Zarif strode into the dining room, Ella spared him a careless glance of acknowledgement. 'Oh, it's you,' she said in the same voice with which she might have greeted an unappetising serving of cold porridge.

'I said some things I should not have said,' Zarif announced.

'How's that new?' Ella asked waspishly, watching his long, beautifully shaped fingers flex across the chair back in angry response and getting a mean kick from that tiny display of human frailty. 'Apparently you think I am calculating and mercenary, and someone who wants to stay a queen and spend loads and loads of your money.'

'Instead of which you are the heartbreak of the Qurzah shopkeepers because you browse and never buy. I know that material things are not important to you,' Zarif told her tautly, 'but from this moment on we are truly man and wife with all that that entails and it is permanent.'

Ella stared stonily at the jug of hot chocolate whose fumes now made her tummy roll as though she were on the deck of a storm-tossed ship. *'Permanent?'* she queried half an octave higher. 'No, thanks. I still want the divorce I was promised.'

Zarif stared back at her in stark disbelief, darkly fringed tawny eyes full of condemnation. 'You can't have a divorce now...you're *pregnant.*'

'And yet you are *not* a happy camper about that,' Ella slotted in drily, ramming back her sense of pained rejection as she made that observation. 'So, please don't think for one moment that I intend to ruin both our lives, and our child's for that matter, by staying with you as your wife *for ever*. On those terms for ever sounds like a death sentence.'

Zarif straightened to his full imposing height. 'Even if I have to lock you up and throw away the key, understand one thing now...' he advised harshly. 'I will not lose *another* child.'

Jolted out of self-pitying sarcasm by that very real statement of loss, Ella pushed herself up out of her seat with a troubled frown. 'Zarif?'

'My son died as a stranger to me,' Zarif bit out not quite steadily, shocking her where she stood from the pain he made no attempt to hide, lean, dark features stamped with lines of grief and regret he had never allowed her to see before. 'I held him only once and briefly after his birth. Then he was kept away from me because men were not welcome in the nursery. It wasn't thought proper or normal for me to take too much of an interest in him while he was still a baby. I was told I could get to know my son later when he was older...but there *was* no later and he never *did* get any older...'

And Ella's heart cracked right down the middle inside her, tears on his behalf stinging her eyes and clogging her throat. She hurt so much for him at that moment that she almost crossed the room to wrap her arms round him in a desperate effort to comfort him. 'I'm so sorry, Zarif,' she said weakly instead.

'That is why I will not let you leave me or take my child away from me. Boy or girl, it is immaterial. I will *be* here for this child at every stage of his or her life,' he completed hoarsely.

'I completely understand how you feel,' she whispered and she honestly did. He had lost his infant son and her talk of divorce had made him feel threatened and, of course, if she were to take their child back to the UK, he would see little of him or her, so his concern and fear on that score were perfectly understandable.

'Then understand that I will not let you go,' Zarif repeated doggedly. 'We will stay married and, if need be, we will *work* at staying married.'

Ella lost colour, wondering if he would need to work that hard to live with her as his wife. Would he be constantly wishing she were Azel? Wishing she were a woman from his own culture? Longing for a break from her? Wishing he could occasionally ring the changes by taking another woman to his bed?

Exactly how would it feel to be granted the status of being a for-ever wife purely and simply because she had given birth to his baby? She believed that the burden of being essentially unwanted would crush her spirit. She wanted him to want her, didn't she? She always had. She thought of her clumsy seduction attempt the night before when she had been thrilled by his response and her face burned hot. Sadly, Zarif was not saying anything she wanted to hear and he never would, would he?

He hadn't wanted or planned a child with her. He hadn't chosen her as the mother of his child. He had chosen her to share his bed, to provide light entertainment and sexual satisfaction within the respectable guise of marriage. But he hadn't ever wanted a *real* marriage with her, had he? And why did that hurt so much? Why did all her emotions feel raw-edged? Why did she feel so desperate and despairing?

Because she wanted more from him, had always wanted *more* from the instant she looked at him at the tender age of seventeen and fell head over heels in love for the one and only time in her life. And now she was looking at Zarif afresh and with much greater maturity and the sudden sinking acknowledgement that she still loved Zarif al-Rastani with all her heart and her soul. No other man had ever stirred her brain or her body the way he did, no other man could hurt her so easily. Pride had made her tell herself that she had got over him but she had been lying to herself all along. Unrequited love could have tremendous sticking power.

'What I don't understand,' Ella admitted thinly, 'is that three years ago you wanted to marry me and yet now you're behaving like you've been trapped by some designing hussy! What changed?'

'You said no,' Zarif growled like a grizzly bear.

A great storm of fiery emotion engulfed Ella, who was thoroughly sick of his inability to work out the obvious. 'Of course I said no. I was madly in love with you and then you told me you still loved Azel and that she was irreplaceable—'

His brilliant dark eyes narrowed as he stared back at her in evident bewilderment. 'I'm sure I did not say that.'

'You *did* say it. You said she would always be in your heart and only a total madwoman would have married you after being told that!'

'You said you were madly in love with me...' he breathed uncertainly.

'Three years ago...before I wised up and re-alised that you were a lost cause better left lost in the past!' Ella parried with hot cheeks and acid bite as she stalked past him.

Zarif was frozen in the centre of the room try-ing to recall saying what she had flung at him. Had his guilty conscience stirred him into mak-ing that claim? Could he really have been that crass that day? Was it possible that Ella had loved him then? A flicker of gold burned in his ab-stracted gaze as he mulled that idea over until it burst like a rainbow on a sunny day over his every thought. *Inshallah*, he had been blessed by the gift of another child and the perfect excuse to keep the woman of his dreams. Did he really need that excuse? What had he been agonising about? And why had he driven her away?

Even his uncle had urged him to move on and recognise that this was a fresh start. But he hadn't moved on, had he? He had allowed his guilt and regret from the past to wall him off from the infinitely more promising present. It was time to tell her the truth even if that threatened to change her view of him in a way that he dreaded. Swallowing hard, Zarif headed to his office safe. Pride was all very well but his marriage was on the line and he did not think he was in a strong enough position to keep secrets.

CHAPTER ELEVEN

ELLA WAS SO angry and wounded that she wanted to scream her hurt to the rooftops. Zarif wanted the baby but he didn't want her.

Ella would only be tolerated and accepted as a wife because she was the baby's mother. Zarif would continue to view Azel as the perfect matchless partner even while Ella lay in his bed and gave birth to his child. It wasn't fair, it simply wasn't fair, she thought with ferocious resentment even though she knew that life was frequently unfair. She could not face leading such a life with Zarif even for the sake of their unborn child. Such a marriage could not possibly be happy and their child would be damaged by the strife between them. He *had* to divorce her. Somehow she had to persuade him that a divorce that would grant him liberal access to their child was the best solution for all of them.

Of course, she could do something scandalous, which would make it much easier for him to accede to a divorce, she conceded, her brain roving off on a tangent as she descended a rear set of stairs in search of fresh air. She was desperate to escape the palace and leave behind the hothouse tension of her row with Zarif. It was running away and she knew it was running away but she couldn't face another session with Zarif, particularly not after having exposed herself to the extent that she had. Why had she told him that she had been madly in love with him three years earlier? What had she hoped to achieve with that admission? In retrospect she felt humiliated but knew she had brought it on herself.

As the heat engulfed her in an area not cooled by fans, Ella longed for a breeze and thought nostalgically back to the occasion when her father had taken her mother and her out for a drive in an open-topped sports car. Of course, if she wanted to scandalise the populace she could go for a drive now, she thought suddenly, thinking of the vast basement of high-performance cars she had viewed only the week before when she was exploring the palace. Zarif might rarely drive himself anywhere but he had a fabulous collection of vehicles. Her chin rising at a combative angle, Ella crossed the courtyard to the garage block.

It was the work of a moment to indicate which car she wanted brought out to the two men engaged in lovingly polishing one. Naturally they didn't question the command: she was Zarif's queen and they undoubtedly assumed that he or someone else would be driving her.

Within minutes, the fire-engine-red Ferrari was parked out on the forecourt, paintwork gleaming in the hot sunlight. Ella breathed in deep and slow and got behind the wheel. It was a very powerful car. As she drove towards the gates she travelled slowly while she familiarised herself with the steering and the controls. There was no way she would take it into the city centre, she conceded, shrinking from the prospect of all that traffic, but she could certainly take it for a spin on the desert highway that encircled the walls of the old city.

The gate guards made no attempt to hide their

shock when they saw her seated behind the wheel driving and without a team of bodyguards in tow. Obedience, however, was engrained in the royal staff and they opened the gates, although she had not the smallest doubt that the minute she drove out the guards would be on the phone informing the powers-that-be that she had left the grounds and, even worse, was breaking the law by driving herself. Indeed she had only travelled a couple of hundred yards before she glanced in her rearview mirror and saw two army vehicles hurtling out onto the road behind her. The sight made her foot press down on the accelerator.

'Your wife has just driven out of the gates in your Ferrari!' Hamid informed Zarif, huffing and puffing and red-faced from the speed with which he had mounted the stairs to deliver that explosive news.

Cold sweat drenched Zarif at the thought of Ella behind the wheel of so powerful a car. He closed his eyes and for a split second he prayed, warding off the images of the aftermath of Azel's fatal crash, the wreckage scattered across the road, the poignant sight of his son's tiny jacket lying by the roadside covered in sand.

'I must follow her.'

'I have put the army in pursuit.'

Zarif spun in disbelief. 'Are you crazy? I don't want anyone chasing her, panicking her into crashing!' he exclaimed in horror. 'Tell them to keep their distance from her and not to try to stop her because I don't want her speeding up to escape them.'

Hamid was already on the phone muttering fervent apologies, regretful eyes locked to Zarif, who was already racing for the stairs and the fastest means of transport he possessed.

Ella was relieved that the army escort stayed well back from her. Two cars loaded with teenagers, however, overtook the Ferrari. They waved and honked horns noisily, poked their heads through their sun roofs to take photos of her and, even though she was deliberately driving slowly to be safe, Ella was childishly affronted at being overtaken in Zarif's high-performance car.

On her first loop of the city walls, she glimpsed

a police car parked at the entrance to the old city with its roof light flashing and it was at that point that two other cars fell in behind her. She peered in the rear-view mirror, registering that the nearest car definitely had a female driver at the wheel, and she grinned. Without warning, the police car appeared on the road behind her, travelling at great speed to overtake her, and she was about to pull off the road feeling that she had made her point when the police car simply moved into the lane in front of her, slowing her down but taking up pole position.

Hamid was on the phone to Zarif, who was airborne. 'Women are pouring out of the shops and the offices and getting behind car wheels all over the city to follow the Queen's car. It's turning into a mass demonstration on the desert highway and the police and the army say there is a danger of public disorder and they want to arrest everybody involved.'

'No woman is to be stopped or arrested,' Zarif decreed. 'Interference would only raise the risk of an accident occurring.'

'My wife is out there in a car too,' Hamid confided in a small voice.

'We married gutsy women, Hamid. They have a good side and a bad side, or should I call it an exciting side?' Zarif sighed, trying to work out how best to get Ella off the road safely.

He could not phone her. He would not *risk* phoning her. Azel had been on the phone when she crashed.

The noise of hundreds of car horns blaring made Ella look in the rear-view mirror and she almost jumped on the brakes because there was a whole procession of cars following her. Overhead she could hear more than one helicopter hovering. Swallowing hard, she drove on behind the leading police car, wishing they would step on it a bit. She was ready to head back to the palace. She had made her statement but she had not intended to cause traffic chaos or involve other women in her protest.

It was a stupid sexist law and it ought to be changed but she didn't want to get anyone else into trouble. She looked on in disbelief as a pickup truck with a large film camera mounted on the back overtook the police and what she assumed to be the news crew proceeded to film the parade of cars. It was a very dangerous manoeuvre, which convinced Ella that it was time for her to wind down the tension by quietly bowing out.

Ella pulled off the road onto the stony, sandy desert plain. Her army escort followed. Before she could even climb out of the Ferrari a ring of soldiers surrounded the vehicle and there was the truly deafening noise of a helicopter landing nearby. The car horns were still going like mad. Barely a minute later, the ring of soldiers parted and Zarif strode towards her, his lean, breathtakingly beautiful face taut and informative.

Anxiety exploded inside Ella. She had done what she had done. It was a senseless law and she had made a mockery of it but she had not realised that she might inspire other women into staging a massive demonstration alongside her. That made her feel guilty. That was more of a lesson than she had intended to teach and, although she had known her protest would embarrass Zarif, she was suddenly not proud of what she had evidently achieved. In fact the huge fuss and the pull on resources that her simple drive had created suddenly made her feel ashamed and about one inch tall.

'Zarif...' she began hesitantly.

Without a word he bent down and scooped her bodily up into his strong arms and carted her back to the helicopter he had evidently landed in. He settled her into the passenger seat and did up the safety belt in a series of silent determined movements.

'You're furious with me,' she breathed shakily.

'No, I was more afraid for your safety in the mood you were in,' Zarif contradicted. 'I'm a natural worrier... Azel and my son died on that same stretch of road.'

Ella turned pale. 'I'm so sorry...I didn't think.'

His strong jaw line clenched. 'She was a new driver. I told her that she needed more practice before she took to the road but she was determined to meet me at the airport. She was on the phone, something may have distracted her...possibly the baby. We'll never know. She crashed head-on into a truck. And because of a tragedy that could have been foreseen, Halim drew up an unjust law forbidding women from driving. It was the only law he put forward in all his years as Regent and, in the light of what had happened to his daughter and grandson, nobody had the heart to say no to him,' he proffered heavily as he vaulted back out of the helicopter and stood by the door talking to her. 'But *I* should've had the strength to oppose him. When I saw all those women driving behind you, determined to show solidarity with you, I finally realised what a huge source of resentment that law has become. Regardless of how Halim feels about it, the law will be removed from the statute books as soon as possible. The taxi drivers will be furious but there are always losers in every scenario.'

Slamming the door on her, Zarif strode round the nose of the helicopter and climbed into the pilot's seat.

'You're flying us?' she prompted in surprise.

'I've been flying for many years,' Zarif told her gently.

'I didn't know,' she said as he fiddled with the controls and spoke into the radio.

'Changing the law is the right thing to do,' she

told him as the whine of the whirling rotor blades began. 'But it wasn't fair for me to do something like that in public to embarrass you.'

'I wasn't embarrassed. I was surprisingly proud of you for standing up for what you believed in,' Zarif admitted with a sidelong glance at her from black-fringed dark eyes. 'Why did you pull off the road and stop it?'

'When that film crew thrust their vehicle in front of us, I realised it was getting dangerous and I didn't want anyone to get hurt. How the heck did people find out about what I was doing so fast?'

'It was plastered all over Facebook and Twitter within minutes of you leaving the palace. You're a heroine now. Why did you do it?' he shot at her loudly and abruptly when they were airborne.

'I thought it would make you divorce me and that that would be for the best.'

'Never!' he rebutted succinctly and that was the last word exchanged for some time.

They landed in the desert, the *real* desert, which she had only seen in pictures, a place of deep rolling golden dunes and grey rocky outcrops, and it was like stepping out into a cocoon of unbelievable heat. 'Where on earth are we?' she asked as Zarif lifted her out of the passenger seat.

'Honeymoon Central,' Zarif quipped as he tucked something that might have been a book under one arm.

'I beg your pardon?' Ella gasped, her head whipping round as she stared in disconcertion at the great steep-walled and turreted grey fortress built on top of the stony hill that lay directly ahead of them.

'The Old Fort, once used as a hunting lodge, latterly as my grandparents' holiday home. It was a special place for them,' Zarif told her. 'There's a long route in by road and our luggage will be coming in that way tonight.'

'We're going to *stay* here?' Ella queried in bewilderment, worry stirring that this could be the first step in his threat to lock her up and throw away the key. Would he really maroon her in this remote place on her own?

'Yes, until we get everything ironed out between us. It's peaceful here and there are no distractions,' Zarif pointed out smoothly as he stood back for her to precede him up the flight of steps carved out of the rock face. 'You go first and take your time because it's a long climb. We're not in a hurry.'

She was so out of breath that he had to carry her up the last flight of steps. At the top she found herself in a surprisingly pretty cobbled courtyard. Urns overflowed with colourful flowers in the shade below the arches. An old gardener was watering the plants in a corner bed and he greeted Zarif with a toothless smile and a very low bow.

The solid wooden doors of the entrance already stood open on a wonderfully cool blue and white tiled hallway. 'This is very pretty and not at all what I expected from the outside of this place,' Ella confided.

'My grandmother renovated it. I'm afraid it's a little old-fashioned now,' Zarif warned, urging her into an elegant salon furnished very much in the British style. The curtains and the paintings and the wallpaper all looked sadly faded but a gracious atmospheric charm remained.

'You never told me how your grandmother met

and married your grandfather,' she remarked, perching on a window seat to catch her breath.

'She and her father were hired to conserve the library at the old palace where we used to store many very old and valuable documents. Now they're in the latest temperature-controlled environment in the new palace. For my grandfather, Karim, it was a case of love at first sight. Her name was Violet,' Zarif divulged. 'But Violet refused to have anything to do with him because he kept a harem full of concubines.'

'Oh, my word, even I didn't have an excuse to say no that was that good!' Ella could not resist gasping.

'He offered to reduce the harem by half.'

'Whoopy-do!' Ella carolled, unimpressed.

'Then he endowed all his concubines with dowries and found them husbands and thought that Violet would finally agree to be his.'

'And she didn't?'

'No, she wanted the assurance that she would be his one and only wife because, of course, the Qu'ran allows a Muslim four. The council were very much against him giving such an undertaking before there was proof that Violet could give him children but Karim rebelled and went ahead and married her.'

'And were they happy?' Ella prompted.

'Very much so and that, you must understand, is the example that I grew up with. A happy loving marriage conducted very much in the Western style. Violet was a daredevil. She jumped out of aeroplanes, raced camels and deep-sea dived. She would have driven that car today just like you did. And she would have stopped for the same reason.' Zarif's lean dark face shadowed. 'Yet she and Karim, who had such a caring relationship, thrust me into an arranged marriage as a teenager. It was a done deal to unite the two different factions in Vashir. Those who preferred Halim's conservatism to the risk of the unknown rule of a young man, who was the son of an absentee Vashiri princess and an Italian playboy.'

Ella was tense and afraid of saying something that might offend but she was finally beginning to suspect that Zarif's marriage had not been as idyllic a match as he had led her to assume. 'But your marriage worked, didn't it?'

'After a fashion,' Zarif conceded uncomfortably. 'It was far from ideal.'

'But you *loved* her,' Ella reminded him staunchly, not wanting him to try and deny that truth for the sake of soothing her feelings of jealousy.

'Not in the way Azel wanted me to love her. I loved her as a childhood playmate, a cousin.' His expressive mouth curled and he lifted his hands in a sudden violent gesture of frustration. 'How can I tell you the truth *without* betraying her memory?' Zarif spun away from her before continuing harshly. 'To me, she felt more like a sister than a wife because we spent too many years being raised together in her father's home. There was no chemistry, no romance. I didn't *want* to marry her but I did my duty to the best of my ability.'

Ella was so shocked by that admission that she literally stared at him with wide incredulous eyes. 'I thought you adored her...'

'She was my best friend and very supportive,' Zarif hastened to assure her. 'But I could not return her idealised feelings for me and that made me feel very guilty. I felt as though I was taking all the time while she did all the giving.'

'But if she gave that was *her* choice,' Ella whispered. 'And if she loved you she may well have been content.'

'She was content but I was not happy with her,' Zarif confessed in a ragged and reluctant confession. 'I hid it as best I could. I would have done anything rather than hurt her. But I was always aware that there was a big empty pit of nothingness at the centre of our marriage and the one thing we could have shared...our son, she preferred to keep to herself.'

Ella stared steadily back at him. 'So, if you weren't that happy with her, why did you go out of your way to stress how much you loved her three years ago?'

'Blame my guilty conscience for that piece of foolishness. I *was* sincerely devastated when she died. That was the main reason why I left Vashir to study abroad. I needed a change of scene and the chance to occupy my brain, but that is not what I ultimately found there,' Zarif told her flatly.

'I don't think I want to talk about the past any more,' Ella admitted ruefully. 'I think our current troubles are very much of the present.'

'I should have told you how happy I am about the baby,' Zarif replied instantly, resting tawny eyes on her with extraordinary intensity. 'Yes, I was shocked but I do very much want our child.'

Ella sighed. 'I never doubted that, Zarif.'

'But you *do* doubt that I want to retain you as my wife. And yet I have *always* wanted you, *habibti.*' Zarif withdrew the object she had assumed was a book from below his arm and set it on the coffee table where she could see that it was a leather-bound photo album. 'It shames me to show you this but I hope that revealing one of my biggest secrets to you will persuade you that I am telling you the truth.'

Ella was frowning. 'What secret?' she questioned.

Zarif bent down and flipped open the photo album at random and she stood up to approach, recognising even from a distance of several feet that she was looking at a photograph of her younger self. She was wearing jeans and a sweater, walking along the street beside Cathy. 'Who took that and when?' she demanded in bewilderment.

'I paid someone to take a collection of discreet photos of you when you were eighteen. It was… my secret stash. I could not have you—you were too young for me. I needed something and the photos were the only consolation I dared to take,' he framed with a ragged edge to his deep drawl. 'The first time I saw you was the first weekend Jason brought me to your home with him. You were seventeen and in the garden with your mother. You were wearing shorts and a pink top and you were laughing and you were literally the most beautiful sight I had ever seen. I was obsessed from that moment on…'

Ella was stunned by that speech. 'I don't believe you,' she told him bluntly even though she remembered that same first meeting. He might have said she was a beautiful sight but her memory was different. She had been mortified that a very hot and fanciable male should see her in shorts that she was convinced showed far too much of her chubby thighs and bottom.

She reached for the album and flicked through it, finding photo after photo taken without her awareness. She was shocked, disbelieving.

'Let's face it—I behaved like a stalker,' Zarif breathed, dark blood lining his spectacular cheekbones. 'I have no excuse.'

'But you *never* showed the slightest interest in me!' Ella reminded him helplessly.

'I couldn't. You were still at school when we first met. I had to wait for you to grow up and exist on very occasional glimpses of you,' Zarif countered grimly. 'It was an obsession that didn't fade. I didn't want any other woman. I waited for you.'

Ella viewed him wide-eyed. 'You waited *four* blasted years for me to grow up?' she prompted. 'Were you crazy? I wanted you too! Eighteen would have been fine!'

'No. I wanted a woman, not a child, which is why I waited. I didn't want to take advantage of your inexperience. I didn't want hero worship. I didn't want to turn your head with my money. I just wanted you,' Zarif breathed emotively. 'But what I didn't appreciate then, because I had never felt that way before, was that I was not simply attracted you, I was in love with you.'

'Oh, no, please don't tell me that now three years *too late!*' Ella suddenly framed in anguished reproach. 'If you loved me when you proposed and I turned you down it will break my heart because I loved you too.'

'But it was my fault. I screwed up back then. And even after demanding this second chance with you I screwed up again so badly that I honestly didn't know how to convince you of the duration and strength of my feelings for you without showing you that embarrassing album of stolen photos,' Zarif told her in a hoarse undertone. 'I felt such guilt that I was unable to love Azel. How could I admit that within two years of her death I took one look at a seventeen-year-old girl and fell in love with her?'

'You loved me and you *lied* about it, you idiot!' the woman of Zarif's dreams hurled at him in a tone of tragedy.

'Yes, *habibti*…when it comes to the love stuff, I'm pretty useless,' Zarif was willing to admit because it gave him the chance to sweep her up into his arms and hold her so close that she could barely breathe. 'But I *do* love you. I love you so much that I don't think I could live without you now.'

'But *you* said—' Ella began.

'No, don't remind me. We both said lots of things that day—like you telling me that women in Vashir are treated like second-class citizens.'

Ella reddened. 'It was the driving-ban thing. I didn't know what it was really like until I lived here. I didn't mean to insult you. I was just trying to think up excuses. I couldn't tell you the truth and you seemed to feel nothing at all for me—you were so cold, so emotional.'

'I was very upset. I was genuinely expecting you to say yes. That was arrogant of me. But then I didn't know how I really felt about you until you told me about the baby and suddenly I realised that I was glad of *any* excuse to keep you.'

'An excuse?' she gasped.

'And then I asked myself why I needed an excuse to do what I wanted to do, which was keep you for ever,' Zarif extended abstractedly, studying her lovely face with warm dark golden eyes of appreciation. 'And that's what I intend to do if you'll let me...keep you for ever.'

'I can't believe that you've loved me all this time,' Ella admitted apologetically.

'I will teach you to believe it, *habibti*,' Zarif swore as he carried her up the narrow staircase and across a wide landing into a shaded bedroom. 'But first, since there should be no more secrets between us, there are some other things I must talk about.'

He loved her? Could she believe that? She could certainly understand his guilt over his inability to love the first wife who had patently loved him. She could understand why he had been unable to admit that and why it would have been much easier for him to credit that his reaction to Ella was simple lust. 'Am I the only person you've ever been in love with?'

'Yes, *habibti*.'

'That's unusual,' she pronounced, trying to take a sensible attitude as he set her down on a bed made up with snowy white linen. 'Although you're the only person I've ever been in love with as well.'

'As my grandmother would have said were she here now, we're a match made in heaven, *habibti*,' Zarif declared with tender amusement. 'You came back into my life to save me from a lifetime of regret, and loneliness.'

'No,' Ella corrected. 'I came back into your life to ask you for a favour—'

'And I was a total bastard,' Zarif said softly, carrying her hand to his lips and pressing a kiss to her palm in mute apology for that meeting at the hotel. 'I was very bitter when you turned me down three years ago. I thought you had deliberately lured me into proposing just for the ego boost of blowing me off.'

Ella was shaken. 'But I wouldn't have done that to anyone!'

'I was bitter,' Zarif repeated doggedly. 'Angry, desperately unhappy. I wanted you so much, believed you were about to become my wife and then, suddenly, I couldn't have you.'

'You'd have got me with bells on if you'd told me you loved me then. Of course you didn't appreciate that what you were feeling was love or you wouldn't have wittered on about Azel,' she worked out for herself, her lovely face reflective. 'But maybe on some level after your first marriage you just weren't ready to make such a major commitment to me and maybe I was still too immature.'

'I'm trying to make excuses for the way I behaved after you turned me down,' Zarif confessed grittily. 'I went off the rails for a while… sex, alcohol.'

Ella quirked a fair brow. 'Loose women?'

As she studied Zarif he flinched and reddened with embarrassment. 'All blonde, all blue-eyed. I tried to fantasise every one of them into being you,' he groaned. 'My brothers thought it was good for me to live like that for a while and that it would have been foolish of me to get married again so soon and tie myself down.'

'But what did *you* think?' Ella pressed, pained by what he was telling her, although it really wasn't anything she hadn't expected when she had seen photos of him in clubs and at parties with glamorous women.

'I would have exchanged all of the partying for one day married to you. It was sleazy and

I'm ashamed of it but for a long time afterwards I blamed you for having set me off on that path by…hurting me.' He found it so difficult to get that confession of vulnerability past his lips that he almost choked on that word.

Ella hated to think that she had hurt him but then he had hurt her as well and that was what happened when two people didn't understand each other or their feelings. Slowly she laced her small fingers with his long tense ones, recognising what it had cost his pride to speak as freely as he had done about both the duration of his love and his mistakes, and loving him all the more for that sacrifice. 'We're all good at blaming others for our mistakes, and at least I know you've satisfied any curiosity you had about that kind of lifestyle. As for the apartment in Dubai—'

Zarif tensed. 'I'll sell it. I could never take you there.'

'So, we draw a line under it and put it *all* behind us, no more recriminations, no more shame or regrets. Stop beating yourself up about your blunders. It's the past,' she emphasised with quiet assurance. 'We'll make a wonderful future to-gether for our child.'

'A future in which you occasionally throw yourself at me again?' Zarif whispered wickedly.

Ella pushed him flat on the bed. 'For the last time, I did not *throw* myself at you!'

'I loved every second of it,' her husband admitted shamelessly, shooting her an irreverent grin that lit up his lean, darkly devastating features and made her heart leap inside her chest.

'When's your birthday?' she asked him.

'That's months away!' Zarif groaned as he drew her down and extracted a very long and passionate kiss from her lush mouth.

Supporting herself on one hand, Ella traced teasing fingers along the line of a long, powerful thigh and watched him jerk taut. 'I'm not sure I could wait that long either. I love you so much, Zarif, but from now on you have to tell me that you love me at least once every day.'

He sat up and peeled off his robe and the shirt beneath in one potent and impatient movement, revealing his golden muscular torso. 'I love you, *habibti.*'

Ella felt incredibly powerful when he looked at her with his heart in his beautiful eyes. 'I love you too.'

Ella twisted and turned to get a good view of her outfit. Brought as a gift from her mother-in-law, Mariyah, the sleek sapphire-blue evening gown oozed Italian chic.

'It looks amazing,' Cathy told her cheerfully.

Ella turned to smile at her childhood friend. 'Fine feathers make fine birds.'

'No, it's the jaw-dropping sapphire jewels, not the dress, that knocks the eyes out first,' Soraya teased. 'But even when you're in jeans, you look great, Ella. You've kept your figure so well.'

But the baby weight had been an uphill challenge to shed, Ella reflected wryly. She had managed it twice, however, and now, and quite unexpectedly, she was going to have to do it again, but that was still a secret. 'There's still lumps and bumps in places there didn't used to be,' she lamented.

Five years of marriage and two children, Ella mused in wonder, because the time had flown and seemed to speed up with every passing month. Halim had only passed away eighteen months ago and Zarif still missed the older man a great deal. His mother, Mariyah, had gradually become a more frequent visitor, who took great pleasure in her grandchildren.

Given the opportunity, she had talked frankly to Zarif about why she had handed him over so completely to his grandparents. Mariyah had known that she had no father figure to offer her son and had deemed her own father preferable to the risks of Gaetano Ravelli's potential influence. She had called herself selfish for wanting to pursue a career, which she could never have had in those days had she returned to Vashir, but she had believed it would be even more selfish to deprive Zarif of his heritage and very probably the chance to become King. Mother and son had made their peace and, although they might never be especially close, they were becoming friends and Zarif valued the connection.

Ella's parents were frequent visitors in common with Zarif's brothers. Ella and Zarif had seen Jason occasionally when they visited her home but contact had been minimal. Jason had narrowly escaped a jail sentence two years earlier and had been put on probation when he became marginally involved with a pyramid selling scheme that broke the law. Since then Jason had been working in a sales role for a national company and Ella suspected that Zarif had somehow fixed that job for her brother behind the scenes, either because he felt sorry for him or because he felt sorry for the worry and distress Jason caused their parents. In recent times, however, her brother had not been a cause for concern and Ella was starting to dare to hope that he had learned his lesson and was prepared to turn his life around.

As for Ella, she was still head over heels happy in her marriage. When she and Zarif wanted alone time, they flew out to the Old Fort for a few days. Now it was their fifth anniversary and they were having a giant weekend party at the old palace attended by all their family and friends.

Cathy was now a mother as well with a toddler and she ran the thriving bookshop with her husband, since Ella had surrendered her share of the business. Soraya had had twin girls the previous year and had barely paused in her hectic career schedule. Ella and Soraya had become close friends while working together on the opening of the royal museum. Although the exhibits closely followed the rise of the al-Rastani dynasty, the central focus had become the history and civilisation of Vashir, which Ella had come to love almost as much as she loved her husband. But then she didn't think she could ever love anything or anybody as much as she loved Zarif and their children.

Her ears pricked up as she heard a distant roar from the courtyard.

'Your husband is home,' Soraya remarked with a grin.

Through the doors open onto the stone balcony beyond the window, Ella could hear Zarif laying down the law to their sons, Hatim and Murad. Hatim was a boisterous and daring little boy and his little brother, a scant eighteen months his junior, tended to follow him slavishly into mischief. 'A little military-style discipline keeps the boys in order,' she confided.

She heard Zarif's steps on the stairs and her face lit up as she instinctively looked towards the doorway.

'It's like *Romeo and Juliet* round here *every day*,' Cathy muttered appreciatively as she caught that look.

Zarif strode in and lowered the two little boys clinging to him like monkeys to the floor. Evidently the military discipline had not been too tough this time around. 'They were teasing the guards again, playing hide and seek round them, which is very dangerous,' their father said sternly. 'But they have apologised and now they are going to their rooms.'

'Oh, but…right, OK.' Ella bit back what she had been going to say about how overexcited the boys were waiting for their band of cousins to arrive. She had learned the hard way that two very lively boys were a handful and a staff who adored the little princes and could not do enough to please them didn't help.

'*Mum?*' Hatim said pleadingly, a miniature Zarif with flashing tawny eyes and a killer smile.

'Do as your father says,' Ella told him coolly,

hardening herself, knowing that Hatim had to learn about self-control and safety, young though he was. If he wanted to follow in his father's footsteps he had to learn about consequences.

Murad simply burst into floods of inconsolable tears and she could see even Zarif tense against the urge to offer comfort because Murad, cheerful and loving, was that kind of child. But it was Hatim who bent down and took his little brother's hand and patted his back and led him off and Ella was proud of that.

'We'll go downstairs and see how the dinner arrangements are progressing,' Soraya suggested tactfully to Cathy and, with a polite curtsy to Zarif, the two women left the royal couple alone.

'Thanks for not caving in. I could see Murad pushed you close to the edge,' Zarif told his wife with a gleam of appreciation in his beautiful dark golden eyes as he closed the bedroom door. 'They need half an hour to think about what they did and cool off and then they can come out. My brothers and their families have just landed. By the way, is it too late to tell you that you look *amazing*?'

Ella smiled widely at him. 'No.'

'You look amazing but the dress has to come off,' Zarif told her, hauling her close without the smallest warning and kissing her with passionate hunger.

'Be careful with the zip. It's a tight fit,' Ella told him helpfully without a single word of protest. Yes, she would have to redo her make-up and get dressed again but one of the aspects she most loved about Zarif was the strength of his passion for her, his *need* for her.

'I won't have you to myself again until the early hours of the morning…if even then,' Zarif lamented. 'You and Belle and Betsy get talking and sit up half the night.'

'You know you do the same with your brothers…that last holiday we had with Nik and Betsy, you came to bed the first night at dawn.' Skimming off her lingerie with careless hands, Ella lay back naked on the bed but for the famous sapphires and watched her husband strip at even greater speed, enjoying every lithe bronzed and muscular inch of him that emerged from beneath his clothing. Five years hadn't made him any less hot, she thought gratefully.

'And you were in a temper and you got straight back out of bed and now I know what not to do,' Zarif husked, his stunning eyes locked to her lush pale curves with hungry appreciation. 'You're so beautiful, *habibti*.'

'But I'm going to get fat again,' she countered, deciding that it was as good a time as any to break her news.

'*Fat?*' Zarif repeated blankly.

'Cast your mind back to the shower at the Old Fort…no condoms,' Ella reminded him ruefully. 'We thought we'd take the risk—'

'We're pregnant again?' Zarif exclaimed with a huge grin of satisfaction. 'I love it when you're pregnant! That's not fat, that's lush, curvy, *sexy*,' he asserted with rich vocal approval.

Zarif came down on the bed with an even greater hunger for the woman who had transformed his life. He studied her with immense pride and tenderness. 'Maybe this super fertility is a Ravelli thing and we have my father to thank for that one gift.'

'And the "absolutely insatiable for sex" gift? Do we thank him for that too?' Ella asked with a comic roll of her eyes, because she loved the fact that he still couldn't keep his hands off her.

'No, only you do that to me,' Zarif told her, lowering his lithe, aroused length down over her prone body and lowering his head to lick at a perky rosy nipple. 'I could eat you alive at any time of day or night—'

'And frequently *do*.'

'Can't help it…I love you so much, *habibti*,' he murmured with raw sincerity.

And she ran her hands through his luxuriant black hair, framed his spectacular movie-star cheekbones and told him that she loved him too. They were both fully dressed and respectable by the time their guests arrived. Hatim and Murad were released from captivity to mingle with their equally excited cousins and the noise of their games and the rising tide of chatter from their parents rang round the ancient palace walls, giving it more life than it had enjoyed in centuries.

* * * * *

Mills & Boon® Large Print
December 2014

Mills & Boon® Large Print

January 2015

MILLS & BOON®

Why shop at millsandboon.co.uk?

Each year, thousands of romance readers find their perfect read at millsandboon.co.uk. That's because we're passionate about bringing you the very best romantic fiction. Here are some of the advantages of shopping at www.millsandboon.co.uk:

* **Get new books first**—you'll be able to buy your favourite books one month before they hit the shops

* **Get exclusive discounts**—you'll also be able to buy our specially created monthly collections, with up to 50% off the RRP

* **Find your favourite authors**—latest news, interviews and new releases for all your favourite authors and series on our website, plus ideas for what to try next

* **Join in**—once you've bought your favourite books, don't forget to register with us to rate, review and join in the discussions

Visit **www.millsandboon.co.uk**
for all this and more today!